The Witch's Love Spell

Fantasy fiction, Volume 14

Sarah Elizabeth Davis

Published by Arcane Horizons Publishing, 2024.

THE WITCH'S LOVE SPELL

First edition. August 9, 2024.

ISBN: 979-8224526758

Written by Sarah Elizabeth Davis.

Table of Contents

To those who believe in the magic of love, even in the darkest of times.

And to the dreamers who find courage in the face of the unknown,

May your hearts be ever filled with wonder,

And may your love stories be as enchanting as the spells in these pages.

This book is for you.

Chapter 1: The Mysterious Encounter

The Witch's Love Spell

THE SUN DIPPED BELOW the horizon, casting an amber glow over the enchanted forest of Eldoria. Shadows stretched and twisted among the ancient trees, their branches like skeletal fingers clawing at the sky. A symphony of chirping crickets and hooting owls filled the air, blending with the soft rustle of leaves. In the heart of this mystical woodland lived Elara, a young witch whose powers were as potent as her beauty was enchanting.

Elara stood at the edge of a crystalline brook, her reflection rippling in the water's surface. Her long, ebony hair cascaded down her back in waves, and her emerald green eyes sparkled with an otherworldly light. She wore a simple gown of deep green, which matched the hues of the forest, making her almost a part of it. As she hummed a soft melody, the animals of the forest seemed to draw nearer, enchanted by her presence.

For Elara, the forest was home, a place where she could freely practice her magic without fear of persecution. The villagers of Eldoria feared and revered witches, and though they did not venture into the forest, they whispered tales of its guardian witch who kept the forest safe from harm.

As dusk gave way to night, the air grew cooler, and a light mist began to weave its way through the trees. Elara's senses tingled with the familiar presence of magic. She closed her eyes and took a deep breath, feeling the pulse of the forest around her. Tonight, something felt different, as if the forest itself were holding its breath, waiting for something extraordinary to happen.

Meanwhile, in the kingdom of Ravenspire, a young knight named Aiden prepared for his journey. Aiden was known for his bravery and loyalty to the kingdom, his reputation forged in countless battles. With a strong jawline, piercing blue eyes, and a physique honed from years of training, he was the epitome of a knight. His armor, polished to a mirror-like shine, bore the crest of Ravenspire—a black raven with outstretched wings.

Aiden's mission was to deliver a message to a neighboring kingdom, a task he had undertaken with confidence. But as he rode through the forest, the path became less distinct, the trees closing in around him. The air grew thick with an eerie stillness, and soon, he realized he was lost.

"Steady, Shadow," Aiden whispered to his horse, patting its neck reassuringly. The horse neighed softly, sensing its rider's unease. Aiden scanned the dense forest, trying to find any sign of the trail he had been following. But the forest seemed to shift and change, each tree looking the same as the last.

Hours passed, and the sky darkened completely. The moon peeked through the canopy, casting silver beams that danced on the forest floor. Aiden's frustration grew as he navigated the maze of trees, his sense of direction failing him. The sound of distant howls and rustling leaves added to his disquiet, and he tightened his grip on the hilt of his sword.

Just as despair began to creep into his thoughts, a sudden movement caught his eye. A creature, unlike anything he had ever seen, lurked in the shadows. It was large and menacing, with glowing red eyes and a body covered in dark fur. Aiden's instincts kicked in, and he drew his sword, ready to defend himself.

The creature growled and lunged at him with alarming speed. Aiden swung his sword, but the creature dodged and circled him, its eyes locked onto him with a predatory gaze. Despite his training and bravery, Aiden felt a pang of fear. This was no ordinary beast; it was something born of dark magic.

As the creature prepared to strike again, a flash of green light illuminated the forest. The creature yelped in pain and recoiled, its fur singed by the magical energy. Aiden turned to see a young woman stepping out of the shadows, her hands glowing with a mystical aura.

"Stay back!" she commanded, her voice clear and powerful.

The creature hesitated, then snarled and retreated into the darkness, its eyes lingering on Aiden for a moment before vanishing.

Aiden lowered his sword, his heart still racing. "Who are you?" he asked, his voice tinged with both awe and suspicion.

The woman approached, her glowing hands returning to normal. "My name is Elara," she said softly. "I am a witch of this forest."

Aiden's grip on his sword tightened slightly. "A witch?" he repeated, wary. "Why did you save me?"

Elara met his gaze, her emerald eyes calm and steady. "Because you are lost and in need of help," she replied. "And because that creature was not meant to harm anyone. It was corrupted by dark magic, something that does not belong in this forest."

Aiden sheathed his sword, sensing no immediate threat from her. "Thank you," he said, his tone more respectful. "I am Aiden, a knight of Ravenspire. I was on my way to deliver a message, but I lost my way."

Elara nodded, a faint smile touching her lips. "The forest can be tricky to navigate, especially at night. Follow me, and I will guide you to a safe place where you can rest."

Aiden hesitated for a moment but then nodded. He had little choice but to trust her. As they walked, Elara led him through the winding paths of the forest with ease, her presence both comforting and mysterious. The forest seemed to respond to her, the trees parting and the mist lifting as they passed.

They arrived at a small clearing where a cozy cottage stood, illuminated by the soft glow of fireflies. Elara opened the door and gestured for Aiden to enter. Inside, the cottage was warm and inviting, with a fire crackling in the hearth and shelves lined with books and jars of herbs.

"Sit," Elara said, motioning to a chair near the fire. "I will prepare something to help you recover your strength."

Aiden sat down, feeling a wave of exhaustion wash over him. As Elara moved around the cottage, gathering ingredients and brewing a potion, he couldn't help but watch her with a mix of curiosity and admiration. There was something enchanting about her, a grace and strength that intrigued him.

"How long have you lived here?" Aiden asked, trying to make conversation.

"All my life," Elara replied without looking up. "The forest is my home, and its magic is a part of me."

Aiden nodded, taking in his surroundings. "The people of Ravenspire speak of witches with fear and caution," he said. "But you don't seem like the witches from their tales."

Elara smiled gently. "Not all witches are evil, Aiden. Many of us use our magic to protect and heal. The stories you hear are often born of misunderstanding and fear."

She handed him a steaming cup of potion. "Drink this. It will help you feel better."

Aiden took the cup and sipped the potion. It had a surprisingly pleasant taste, a blend of herbs and spices that soothed his tired body. "Thank you," he said, feeling warmth spread through him.

Elara sat down across from him, her expression thoughtful. "Tell me, Aiden, what brings you through the forest at this hour?"

Aiden explained his mission and how he had lost his way. As he spoke, Elara listened intently, her eyes never leaving his. There was a connection between them, an unspoken understanding that seemed to transcend their different worlds.

"You are brave to undertake such a journey," Elara said when he finished. "But the forest is not always kind to those who do not know its ways. You were fortunate to have encountered me."

Aiden smiled wryly. "Fortunate indeed. I owe you my life."

Elara's cheeks flushed slightly. "You owe me nothing, Aiden. It is in my nature to help those in need."

They sat in companionable silence for a while, the fire casting flickering shadows on the walls. Outside, the forest hummed with life, a world of magic and mystery that Elara knew intimately.

As the night deepened, Aiden felt a growing sense of comfort and belonging. Despite the strangeness of his situation, there was something about Elara and her cottage that felt right. He couldn't explain it, but he knew that this encounter was only the beginning of a journey that would change his life forever.

Morning light filtered through the windows, casting a golden glow over the cottage. Aiden woke to the sound of birds singing and the scent of freshly baked bread. He stretched and yawned, feeling more rested than he had in days.

Elara was already up, preparing breakfast. She greeted him with a warm smile. "Good morning, Aiden. I hope you slept well."

Aiden nodded, smiling back. "I did, thank you. Your home is... enchanting."

Elara laughed softly. "I'm glad you think so. Come, eat something before you continue your journey."

They sat together at the small wooden table, sharing a simple but delicious meal. As they ate, they talked about their lives, their dreams, and their fears. Aiden learned more about Elara's life in the forest, her love for nature, and her dedication to protecting it. In turn, he shared stories of his adventures as a knight, his loyalty to Ravenspire, and his desire to make the world a better place.

There was a natural ease between them, a sense of connection that neither had expected. Despite their different backgrounds, they found common ground in their values and their dreams.

As they finished their meal, Elara looked at Aiden with a serious expression. "Aiden, before you leave, there is something you should know."

Aiden's curiosity was piqued. "What is it?"

Elara hesitated for a moment, then took a deep breath. "The creature you encountered last night—it was not an ordinary beast. It was corrupted by dark magic, a magic that is spreading through the forest. I have been trying to find the source, but it is elusive. I fear it may threaten not only Eldoria but also Ravenspire."

Aiden's expression grew grave. "Dark magic? What can I do to help?"

Elara smiled, a glimmer of hope in her eyes. "You have already helped by being here, Aiden. But if you truly wish to aid me, we must work together to uncover the source of this dark magic and put an end to it."

Aiden nodded resolutely. "I will help you, Elara. Whatever it takes."

Elara's smile widened, and she reached out to clasp his hand. "Thank you, Aiden. Together, we can protect both our worlds from this threat."

As they prepared to set out into the forest, Aiden felt a renewed sense of purpose. He had come to Eldoria by chance, but now he knew that his journey had only just begun. With Elara by his side, he felt ready to face whatever challenges lay ahead.

The forest awaited them, a realm of magic and mystery where anything was possible. And as they ventured into its depths, Aiden couldn't help but feel that his encounter with Elara was more than just a twist of fate. It was the beginning of something extraordinary, a bond that would shape the future of both their worlds.

And so, with determination in their hearts and the promise of adventure in their eyes, Aiden and Elara set off together, ready to uncover the secrets of the enchanted forest and the dark magic that threatened it. Their journey had only just begun, but already, it felt like the start of a grand and magical tale.

Chapter 2: The Forbidden Love

The Witch's Love Spell

THE SOFT MORNING LIGHT bathed the forest of Eldoria in a golden hue as Aiden and Elara set out from her cottage. The air was filled with the fresh scent of pine and the sweet aroma of blooming flowers. Birds sang their morning chorus, and the forest seemed alive with anticipation. Aiden's mind was still reeling from the events of the previous night, but he felt a sense of purpose he hadn't experienced in a long time.

As they walked, Elara led the way, her movements graceful and confident. Aiden couldn't help but admire her poise and the way she seemed to blend seamlessly with the natural world around her. He marveled at the way the forest seemed to respond to her presence, as if it recognized her as one of its own.

Background: The History of Witches and Knights

IN THE KINGDOM OF RAVENSPIRE, witches had long been regarded with suspicion and fear. Stories of their dark powers and malevolent intentions were passed down through generations, and knights were trained to hunt and eradicate any witch who posed a threat to the kingdom. This animosity dated back centuries to a time when a coven of powerful witches, led by the malevolent sorceress Morgath, had waged war against the kingdom.

Morgath and her coven had sought to overthrow the monarchy and establish a reign of terror, using their dark magic to summon creatures of the night and cast devastating spells. The knights of Ravenspire, led by the legendary Sir Galen, had fought valiantly to protect the kingdom. After a long and brutal conflict, Sir Galen and his knights had finally defeated Morgath and her coven, sealing them away in a forgotten realm.

Since then, witches were viewed as potential threats, and the memory of Morgath's dark reign cast a long shadow over any who practiced magic. Knights were tasked with upholding the law and ensuring the safety of the kingdom, often clashing with witches who sought to live in peace.

As Aiden and Elara continued their journey, they found themselves growing more comfortable in each other's presence. They talked about their lives, their dreams, and their fears, gradually lowering the walls that had been built by years of mistrust and prejudice.

Conflict: Growing Attraction and Societal Roles

DESPITE THEIR GROWING attraction to one another, both Aiden and Elara were acutely aware of the societal roles that dictated their lives. Aiden, as a knight, had been raised to see witches as enemies, dangerous beings who could not be trusted. Elara, as a witch, had learned to be wary of knights, knowing they were trained to hunt and destroy her kind.

There was a constant tension between them, a dance of emotions that neither could fully understand. Aiden was drawn to Elara's strength and kindness, her unwavering commitment to protecting the forest. Elara, in turn, admired Aiden's bravery and sense of duty, his willingness to help her despite the risks.

One evening, as they sat by a campfire, the conversation turned to their respective roles in the world. Aiden stared into the flames, his expression thoughtful.

"Elara," he began, his voice low, "I can't deny that I feel a connection to you. But I also can't ignore the reality of our situations. As a knight, I've been trained to see witches as a threat. How can we reconcile these differences?"

Elara sighed, her gaze fixed on the flickering fire. "Aiden, I understand your concerns. I, too, have been taught to be cautious of knights. But I believe that not all witches are evil, just as not all knights are cruel. We are individuals, capable of making our own choices. Perhaps we can find a way to bridge the gap between our worlds."

Aiden nodded, appreciating her perspective. "I hope so, Elara. I truly do. But it won't be easy."

Elara smiled faintly. "Nothing worth having ever is."

Inciting Incident: Aiden Discovers Elara's Identity

THEIR JOURNEY CONTINUED, and the bond between them grew stronger. They faced numerous challenges together, from treacherous terrain to magical creatures corrupted by dark forces. Through it all, they supported and protected each other, their mutual respect deepening with each passing day.

One afternoon, they came across an ancient ruin hidden deep within the forest. The crumbling stone walls were covered in moss and ivy, and an air of mystery surrounded the place. Elara's eyes sparkled with curiosity as she approached the entrance.

"This place feels... familiar," she murmured, tracing her fingers along the weathered stone.

Aiden followed her inside, his hand resting on the hilt of his sword. The interior was dimly lit, with shafts of sunlight filtering through gaps in the ceiling. As they explored the ruin, they discovered a chamber filled with old books and artifacts.

Elara's excitement grew as she examined the items. "These are relics of my ancestors," she explained. "Witches who lived here long ago, before the conflict with Ravenspire."

Aiden watched her with a mixture of fascination and concern. "Elara, do you think this place holds any clues about the dark magic we're facing?"

Elara nodded. "It's possible. There may be knowledge here that can help us."

As they continued their search, Aiden noticed a worn leather-bound book on a pedestal. He picked it up and began to read, his brow furrowing as he deciphered the ancient script. The book detailed the history of the coven that once resided in the forest and the powerful spells they had created.

One passage caught his eye, describing a spell known as the "Heart's Bind," a powerful enchantment that could bind two souls together, creating an unbreakable bond of love. Aiden's heart skipped a beat as he realized the implications of such a spell.

"Elara, look at this," he said, showing her the book.

Elara's eyes widened as she read the passage. "The Heart's Bind... it's a rare and powerful spell. It requires immense magical energy and a deep, genuine connection between the two souls."

Aiden's mind raced. Could this spell be the key to overcoming the barriers between them? He looked at Elara, seeing the same mix of hope and uncertainty in her eyes.

That evening, as they set up camp near the ruin, Aiden couldn't shake the thoughts swirling in his mind. He knew that his feelings for Elara were real, but he also understood the gravity of their situation. The Heart's Bind spell could offer a solution, but it was not a decision to be taken lightly.

As they sat by the campfire, Aiden finally spoke. "Elara, I need to tell you something. I've been thinking about the Heart's Bind spell. I believe it could help us, but it also carries great risks."

Elara's expression grew serious. "Aiden, the Heart's Bind is not just a spell. It's a commitment that goes beyond words. If we choose to use it, our souls will be bound together forever. Are you truly prepared for that?"

Aiden looked into her eyes, his resolve unwavering. "Elara, I know the risks, but I also know my heart. I want to be with you, despite the challenges we face. If the Heart's Bind can help us overcome the barriers between our worlds, then I am willing to take that step."

Elara's eyes softened, and she reached out to take his hand. "Aiden, I feel the same way. But we must be certain. The spell requires absolute trust and a genuine connection. If there is any doubt, it could backfire."

Aiden nodded. "I understand, Elara. Let's take our time and make sure this is the right path for us."

The days that followed were filled with introspection and contemplation. Aiden and Elara continued their journey, facing new challenges and deepening their bond. They talked openly about their fears and hopes, their dreams for the future, and the love that was growing between them.

One evening, as they watched the sunset from a hilltop, Elara turned to Aiden, her eyes shining with determination. "Aiden, I believe we are ready. Our connection is genuine, and our hearts are aligned. If you still feel the same, I am willing to perform the Heart's Bind spell."

Aiden's heart swelled with emotion, and he took her hands in his. "Elara, I have never been more certain of anything in my life. Let's do this together."

The following night, under the light of a full moon, Elara prepared for the spell. She drew a circle on the ground with enchanted chalk and placed candles at each cardinal point. The air was thick with magic, and the forest seemed to hold its breath in anticipation.

Aiden stood at the center of the circle, his heart pounding with a mix of excitement and nervousness. Elara joined him, holding a small vial of glowing liquid—the essence needed for the spell.

"Are you ready?" she asked, her voice steady and calm.

Aiden nodded, his eyes locked on hers. "I'm ready."

Elara began to chant, her voice resonating with the power of the forest. The candles flickered, and the circle glowed with a soft, ethereal light. As she continued the incantation, she poured the glowing liquid into her hands and placed them on Aiden's chest, over his heart.

Aiden felt a surge of warmth and energy, a sensation that seemed to envelop his entire being. He closed his eyes, focusing on the connection he felt with Elara.

"By the power of the ancients, I bind our hearts and souls together," Elara intoned. "Let our love be eternal, unbreakable, and true."

As the final words left her lips, a burst of light erupted from the circle, enveloping them both. Aiden felt a rush of emotions, a profound sense of unity and love that transcended anything he had ever experienced.

When the light faded, Aiden opened his eyes to see Elara gazing at him with tears of joy in her eyes. He reached out and gently wiped away a tear, his heart swelling with love.

"It's done," Elara whispered. "We are bound together, Aiden. Our love is eternal."

Aiden pulled her into a tender embrace, his heart overflowing with happiness. "I love you, Elara," he murmured. "And I always will."

Elara smiled, her eyes shining with the same love and devotion. "I love you too, Aiden. Forever."

The days that followed were filled with a newfound sense of purpose and joy. Aiden and Elara faced their challenges with renewed strength, their bond giving them the courage to overcome any obstacle. They continued their quest to uncover the source of the dark magic, their love serving as a beacon of hope in a world filled with uncertainty.

Their journey was far from over, but they knew that together, they could face anything. The forbidden love between a knight and a witch had blossomed into something extraordinary, a love that defied the odds and bridged the gap between their worlds.

And as they walked hand in hand through the enchanted forest of Eldoria, they knew that their love would guide them through whatever lay ahead, their hearts bound together by a spell that was as powerful as the magic of the forest itself.

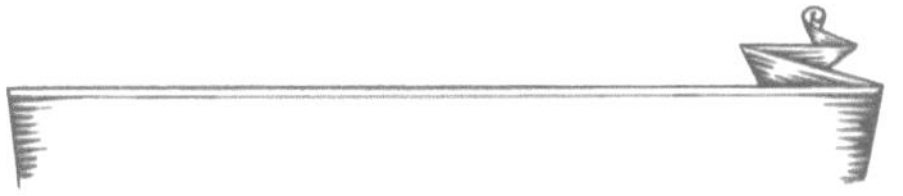

Chapter 3: The Enchanted Amulet

The Witch's Love Spell

THE MORNING SUN FILTERED through the dense canopy of the enchanted forest, casting dappled light on the path where Aiden and Elara walked side by side. Their journey together had already forged a deep bond between them, one strengthened by the recent Heart's Bind spell. But as they ventured further into the heart of Eldoria, they knew that their challenges were far from over.

The forest was alive with magic, its ancient trees whispering secrets and its creatures watching with curious eyes. Every step they took seemed to pulse with an unseen energy, a reminder of the powerful forces that surrounded them.

Magical Element: The Enchanted Amulet

ONE AFTERNOON, AS THEY made their way through a particularly dense thicket, Elara suddenly stopped. Aiden turned to her, noticing the thoughtful expression on her face.

"Is something wrong?" he asked, concern evident in his voice.

Elara shook her head and smiled gently. "No, Aiden. I was just thinking... With the dangers we face, you need more than just your sword and armor for protection."

Aiden raised an eyebrow. "What do you mean?"

Elara reached into a small pouch at her waist and pulled out a beautifully crafted amulet. It was made of silver and shaped like a crescent moon, adorned with intricate runes that seemed to glow faintly.

"This is an enchanted amulet," Elara explained, holding it up for Aiden to see. "It has been passed down through generations of my family. It offers protection against dark magic and enhances the wearer's strength and resilience."

Aiden took the amulet, feeling its cool weight in his hand. He could sense the magic within it, a subtle yet powerful presence. "Are you sure I should have this?" he asked, his voice tinged with awe.

Elara nodded. "Yes, Aiden. I want you to have it. You have proven yourself worthy, and I trust you with it."

With a grateful smile, Aiden placed the amulet around his neck. As soon as it touched his skin, he felt a surge of warmth and energy. The amulet seemed to hum with life, its magic intertwining with his own.

"Thank you, Elara," he said, his voice filled with sincerity. "I will cherish this gift and use it to protect us both."

Elara's eyes sparkled with affection. "I know you will, Aiden. Together, we are stronger."

Bonding: Deepening the Connection

AS THEY CONTINUED THEIR journey, the presence of the enchanted amulet served as a constant reminder of the bond between them. They spent their days navigating the forest, facing challenges and discovering new wonders. Each night, they would sit by the campfire, sharing stories and deepening their connection.

One evening, after a long day of travel, they found a serene glade where they decided to set up camp. The glade was surrounded by towering trees, their leaves rustling softly in the breeze. A small stream babbled nearby, providing a soothing soundtrack to their evening.

As they sat by the fire, Elara noticed Aiden absentmindedly touching the amulet around his neck. "How does it feel?" she asked, curious about his experience with the magical artifact.

Aiden smiled and looked at her. "It feels... comforting. Like a part of you is always with me, protecting me."

Elara's heart swelled with warmth. "I'm glad to hear that. The amulet's magic is strong, but it's your strength and bravery that make it truly powerful."

Aiden reached out and took her hand, his touch gentle and reassuring. "Elara, I can't thank you enough for everything you've done for me. Meeting you has changed my life in ways I never imagined."

Elara squeezed his hand, her eyes filled with emotion. "And you have changed mine, Aiden. I never thought I would find someone who understands and accepts me for who I am. Our bond is something I will always cherish."

They sat in comfortable silence for a while, watching the flames dance and the stars twinkle above. The forest around them seemed to hum with life, as if acknowledging the love that had blossomed between them.

Foreshadowing: Mysterious Visions from the Amulet

AS THE DAYS TURNED into weeks, Aiden began to notice something unusual about the amulet. Whenever he closed his eyes to rest, he would see fleeting visions—images that seemed to come from another world. At first, they were vague and disjointed, but over time, they became clearer and more vivid.

One night, as he lay beside the campfire, he was once again visited by a vision. This time, it was different. He saw a dark forest, shrouded in mist, with twisted trees and shadowy figures moving within. In the center of the forest stood a towering figure cloaked in darkness, its eyes glowing with malevolent intent.

Aiden's heart raced as the vision grew more intense. He saw himself and Elara facing the figure, their expressions filled with determination and fear. The figure raised its hand, and a wave of dark energy surged towards them.

With a gasp, Aiden jolted awake, his body covered in sweat. Elara, who had been keeping watch, immediately rushed to his side.

"Aiden, what happened?" she asked, her voice filled with concern.

Aiden took a moment to catch his breath before answering. "I had another vision, Elara. This one was... different. It felt more real, more urgent."

Elara's brow furrowed. "What did you see?"

Aiden described the vision in detail, his voice steady despite the fear that lingered in his heart. Elara listened intently, her expression growing more serious with each word.

"These visions are not just random images," she said finally. "The amulet is trying to warn us of something. A great danger that we must face."

Aiden nodded. "I believe you're right. But what could it be? And why are we seeing these visions now?"

Elara's eyes darkened with worry. "I don't know, but we must be prepared for whatever lies ahead. The forest holds many secrets, and not all of them are friendly."

The following days were marked by a sense of urgency. Aiden and Elara continued their journey with renewed determination, knowing that they had to uncover the source of the dark magic before it was too late. The visions from the amulet became more frequent and more vivid, each one hinting at a dark future that awaited them.

Despite the looming threat, their bond grew stronger. They faced each challenge together, drawing strength from their love and their shared purpose. Each night, they would sit by the campfire and discuss their plans, their hearts filled with hope and resolve.

One evening, as they sat by the fire, Aiden noticed Elara staring into the flames, her expression pensive. "What's on your mind?" he asked, reaching out to take her hand.

Elara looked at him, her eyes filled with a mixture of determination and fear. "Aiden, I've been thinking about the visions. I believe they are showing us a possible future, one that we must work to change."

Aiden nodded. "I agree. But how do we do that? How do we stop this dark force from overtaking the forest?"

Elara took a deep breath. "We must find the source of the dark magic and destroy it. Only then can we prevent the future we've seen in the visions."

Aiden's grip on her hand tightened. "Whatever it takes, Elara. I will stand by your side and face this danger with you."

Elara smiled, her heart swelling with love and gratitude. "Thank you, Aiden. Together, we can overcome anything."

THE NEXT DAY, THEY set out with renewed determination. The forest seemed to sense their resolve, its ancient magic guiding them towards their goal. As they ventured deeper into the heart of Eldoria, the air grew thicker with enchantment, and the trees seemed to whisper secrets in a language only Elara could understand.

One afternoon, as they made their way through a particularly dense part of the forest, Elara suddenly stopped. Aiden looked at her, noticing the intense focus in her eyes.

"What's wrong?" he asked, his hand instinctively reaching for his sword.

Elara closed her eyes and placed her hand on a nearby tree. "I can feel it," she whispered. "The source of the dark magic. It's close."

Aiden's heart raced with anticipation. "Which way?"

Elara opened her eyes and pointed to a narrow path that wound through the trees. "This way. But be careful, Aiden. The closer we get, the stronger the magic will become."

Aiden nodded, his resolve unwavering. "Let's go."

As they followed the path, the forest grew darker and more foreboding. The trees twisted and gnarled, their branches reaching out like skeletal fingers. The air was thick with a sense of unease, and the sounds of the forest seemed distant and muffled.

After what felt like hours, they emerged into a clearing. In the center stood a massive stone altar, covered in ancient runes and surrounded by a circle of twisted trees. The air crackled with dark energy, and the ground seemed to pulse with a malevolent force.

"This is it," Elara said, her voice barely above a whisper. "The source of the dark magic."

Aiden drew his sword, his eyes scanning the clearing for any signs of danger. "What do we do?"

Elara stepped forward, her hands glowing with a soft, green light. "We must destroy the altar. It is the focal point of the dark magic. Once it is gone, the forest will begin to heal."

Aiden nodded, his grip on his sword tightening. "Let's do this."

As they approached the altar, a chilling wind swept through the clearing, carrying with it a sense of foreboding. The runes on the altar began to glow with a dark, sinister light, and the ground trembled beneath their feet.

Suddenly, a shadowy figure emerged from the darkness, its eyes glowing with malevolent intent. It was the same figure Aiden had seen in his visions, the source of the dark magic that threatened the forest.

"Intruders," the figure hissed, its voice echoing with a dark power. "You dare to challenge me?"

Aiden stepped forward, his sword raised. "We will not let you destroy this forest. Your reign of darkness ends here."

The figure laughed, a chilling sound that sent shivers down their spines. "Fools. You are no match for my power."

With a wave of its hand, the figure summoned a wave of dark energy, sending it crashing towards Aiden and Elara. Aiden raised his sword, the enchanted amulet around his neck glowing with a bright, protective light.

The dark energy collided with the light of the amulet, creating a blinding explosion of magic. Aiden and Elara were thrown back, but they quickly regained their footing, their determination unwavering.

Elara raised her hands, her magic surging with a fierce intensity. "By the power of the ancients, I banish you from this realm!"

The figure snarled, its form flickering as Elara's magic clashed with its own. Aiden charged forward, his sword blazing with the light of the amulet. With a powerful strike, he slashed through the figure's shadowy form, dispelling it with a burst of light.

The figure let out a final, anguished scream before dissolving into darkness. The ground beneath the altar cracked and crumbled, and the dark energy that had surrounded it dissipated.

Aiden and Elara stood in the clearing, their breaths heavy but their hearts filled with triumph. The dark magic had been vanquished, and the forest began to heal, its ancient magic restoring balance to the land.

As the sun set, casting a golden glow over the forest, Aiden and Elara made their way back to the glade where they had set up camp. The amulet around Aiden's neck glowed softly, a reminder of the power of their love and the strength they had found in each other.

They sat by the campfire, their hearts filled with a sense of accomplishment and hope for the future. The challenges they had faced had only strengthened their bond, and they knew that together, they could overcome anything.

Aiden took Elara's hand, his eyes filled with love and gratitude. "Thank you, Elara. For everything."

Elara smiled, her heart swelling with affection. "And thank you, Aiden. Together, we are unstoppable."

As they sat by the fire, the stars twinkling above them, they knew that their journey was far from over. But with their love as their guiding light, they were ready to face whatever challenges lay ahead.

And as the enchanted forest of Eldoria whispered its ancient secrets, Aiden and Elara embraced the future, their hearts bound together by a love that was as powerful and enduring as the magic that surrounded them.

Chapter 4: The Royal Decree

The Witch's Love Spell

The early morning sun cast a golden hue over the kingdom of Ravenspire, its rays illuminating the towering spires of the castle. The castle, a formidable structure of stone and iron, stood as a symbol of strength and authority. Within its walls, the court bustled with activity, knights and nobles discussing matters of state under the watchful eyes of the king.

King Alden of Ravenspire sat upon his throne, a figure of authority and stern resolve. His brow was furrowed as he listened to the latest reports from his advisors. The recent disturbances in the enchanted forest of Eldoria had not gone unnoticed, and rumors of dark magic and witchcraft were spreading like wildfire.

"Your Majesty," an advisor spoke, his voice grave, "we have received reports of increased magical activity in the forest. The people are growing fearful, and there are whispers of witches plotting against the kingdom."

King Alden's expression hardened. "We cannot allow this threat to go unchecked. The safety of Ravenspire is paramount. I will not have my kingdom overrun by witches and their dark magic."

The advisor nodded. "What do you propose, Your Majesty?"

The king rose from his throne, his presence commanding the attention of all in the room. "Issue a royal decree. All knights are to be dispatched to hunt down and eliminate any witch found within the borders of Ravenspire. We will root out this evil and ensure the safety of our people."

A murmur of agreement spread through the court, and the decree was quickly penned and sealed with the royal insignia. The order was clear: witches were to be hunted and eradicated, their presence no longer tolerated within the kingdom.

Conflict Escalation: The Royal Decree

AS THE ROYAL DECREE was announced throughout Ravenspire, it spread fear and panic among the citizens. The stories of witches and their dark magic had always been a source of anxiety, and now, with the king's decree, that fear was being weaponized.

Aiden, who had recently returned to the kingdom after his journey with Elara, was among the knights summoned to the castle. He stood in the grand hall, listening as the decree was read aloud. His heart sank with each word, the weight of his duty pressing heavily upon him.

"Sir Aiden," the king addressed him directly, "you have proven yourself a loyal and capable knight. I trust you to lead the charge in this mission. We must ensure the safety of Ravenspire at all costs."

Aiden bowed, his expression solemn. "Yes, Your Majesty. I will do as you command."

But as he left the castle and prepared for the mission ahead, his mind was in turmoil. The thought of hunting witches, knowing that Elara was among them, filled him with dread. He had seen firsthand the goodness in Elara, her commitment to protecting the forest and the people within it. The idea of turning against her, of seeing her hunted and harmed, was unbearable.

Dilemma: Duty vs. Feelings

AS AIDEN MADE HIS WAY through the bustling streets of Ravenspire, his thoughts were consumed by the impossible choice before him. His duty to the king and the kingdom was clear, but his heart belonged to Elara. The love they had forged in the enchanted forest was real and powerful, and the thought of betraying that love tore at his soul.

He sought solace in the only place that had always brought him peace: the chapel. The small, stone building stood at the edge of the city, a place of quiet reflection and sanctuary. Aiden entered and knelt before the altar, his heart heavy with the weight of his dilemma.

"Father," he prayed, his voice filled with anguish, "guide me in this time of darkness. Show me the path that honors both my duty and my heart."

As he prayed, memories of his time with Elara flooded his mind. He remembered the way she had saved him from the creature in the forest, the way she had trusted him with the enchanted amulet, and the bond they had formed through the Heart's Bind spell. She was not the enemy; she was his ally, his love.

Aiden rose from his knees, a sense of resolve settling over him. He knew what he had to do. He would find a way to protect Elara and the other innocent witches while fulfilling his duty to the kingdom. It would not be easy, but he could not turn his back on the woman he loved.

Tension: Increased Danger

MEANWHILE, IN THE ENCHANTED forest of Eldoria, the atmosphere was one of growing unease. The creatures of the forest sensed the impending danger, their instincts alerting them to the threat that loomed on the horizon.

Elara, too, felt the shift in the air. She had heard whispers of the royal decree, and her heart ached with fear for herself and the other witches who called the forest home. The bond she shared with Aiden through the Heart's Bind spell only heightened her anxiety, as she could sense his turmoil and the difficult choices he faced.

One evening, as Elara gathered herbs near her cottage, she heard the distant sound of hoofbeats. Her heart raced, and she quickly made her way back to the safety of her home. She knew that the knights of Ravenspire would soon be hunting witches, and she had to prepare.

As she entered her cottage, she found herself face-to-face with a familiar figure. Aiden stood in the doorway, his expression a mixture of relief and concern.

"Elara," he said, his voice filled with urgency, "we don't have much time. The king has issued a decree to hunt down witches. You need to leave the forest, find somewhere safe."

Elara's eyes widened with fear and confusion. "Aiden, what are you saying? I can't just abandon my home, my people."

Aiden stepped forward, taking her hands in his. "I know, Elara. But you are in danger. The knights are coming, and they won't stop until they have found and eradicated every witch. I can't let that happen to you."

Tears welled in Elara's eyes as she looked up at him. "Aiden, what about the bond we share? The love we have? I can't leave you."

Aiden's heart ached at her words. "I know, Elara. And I won't let anything happen to you. But you need to trust me. I will find a way to protect you, to protect us. But right now, you need to go."

Elara nodded, her resolve strengthening. "I trust you, Aiden. I will leave, but promise me you'll stay safe too."

Aiden kissed her forehead, his heart heavy with the weight of their parting. "I promise, Elara. We'll find a way through this. Together."

As Elara prepared to leave the forest, Aiden set about his plan to protect her and the other witches. He knew it would be dangerous, but he could not stand idly by while innocent lives were at risk. He would use his position as a knight to gather information and find ways to thwart the witch hunters' efforts.

In the days that followed, the tension in Ravenspire grew. Knights were dispatched to the forest, their mission clear and their resolve unwavering. The people of Ravenspire watched with a mix of fear and anticipation, hoping that the threat of witches would soon be eradicated.

Aiden used his status to stay close to the heart of the operation, gathering intelligence and subtly redirecting efforts to ensure Elara's safety. He became a double agent of sorts, balancing his duty to the kingdom with his loyalty to Elara.

Despite his best efforts, the danger to Elara increased with each passing day. The witch hunters grew more ruthless, their methods more brutal. They left no stone unturned, no forest path unexplored. Aiden's heart pounded with fear each time he ventured into the forest, knowing that Elara's life hung in the balance.

One evening, as Aiden scouted a part of the forest he knew Elara frequented, he heard the distant sound of shouts and clashing steel. His heart raced as he sprinted towards the commotion, his mind filled with dread.

He arrived at a clearing to find a group of knights engaged in battle with a group of witches. The air crackled with magic, and the ground was littered with the bodies of both knights and witches. Aiden's eyes scanned the scene frantically, searching for Elara.

He spotted her at the edge of the clearing, her hands glowing with a fierce green light as she fought off a group of knights. Her expression was one of determination and fear, her eyes blazing with the power of her magic.

Aiden's heart ached at the sight of her in danger. He charged into the fray, his sword flashing as he fought his way to her side. "Elara!" he shouted, his voice cutting through the chaos.

Elara turned, her eyes widening with relief as she saw him. "Aiden!"

Together, they fought off the remaining knights, their combined strength and magic creating a formidable force. As the last knight fell, Aiden and Elara stood panting, their hearts racing with adrenaline and fear.

"We need to get out of here," Aiden said, his voice urgent. "More knights will be coming."

Elara nodded, her eyes filled with worry. "I can't leave the others behind, Aiden. They need me."

Aiden's expression softened. "I know, Elara. But we need to regroup, find a safe place to plan our next move. We can't fight them head-on like this."

Elara sighed, her heart heavy with the weight of her responsibilities. "You're right. Let's go."

They made their way through the forest, their movements quick and cautious. Aiden led them to a hidden cave he had discovered during his scouting missions, a place he hoped would provide temporary sanctuary.

As they settled into the cave, Aiden's mind raced with plans and strategies. They needed to find a way to stop the witch hunters, to protect the witches of Eldoria and ensure their safety. But it would not be easy, and the path ahead was fraught with danger.

In the days that followed, Aiden and Elara worked tirelessly to gather information and plan their next move. They communicated with other witches, warning them of the danger and coordinating efforts to protect their community.

Aiden used his position as a knight to stay informed about the witch hunters' plans, feeding valuable intelligence to Elara and the other witches. He became a beacon of hope and resilience, his love for Elara driving him to fight for a better future.

Despite their best efforts, the tension in the forest continued to escalate. The witch hunters grew more relentless, their methods more brutal. Aiden and

Elara knew that they needed to find a way to turn the tide, to stop the hunters and protect the witches once and for all.

One evening, as they sat by the campfire in the cave, Aiden's mind turned to the enchanted amulet he wore around his neck. The amulet had protected him and guided him through countless challenges, its magic a powerful force in their fight.

"Elara," he said, his voice thoughtful, "the amulet... it has shown me visions, guided us through danger. Perhaps it holds the key to stopping the witch hunters."

Elara looked at him, her expression curious. "What do you mean?"

Aiden reached for the amulet, his fingers tracing the intricate runes. "The visions it has shown me... they have always come true, in one way or another. Perhaps it can show us a way to stop the hunters, to protect the witches and end this conflict."

Elara's eyes sparkled with hope. "It's worth a try, Aiden. The amulet's magic is powerful, and it has guided us this far."

Aiden closed his eyes, focusing on the amulet's magic. He felt a surge of energy, a connection to the ancient power within the artifact. Images began to form in his mind, visions of the future that held the key to their victory.

He saw a hidden chamber deep within the forest, a place of ancient magic and power. He saw himself and Elara standing before an altar, their hands joined as they called upon the magic of the forest to protect their people. He saw the witch hunters defeated, their threat neutralized, and the witches of Eldoria safe once more.

As the vision faded, Aiden opened his eyes, his heart filled with hope and determination. "Elara, I know what we need to do. There is a hidden chamber in the forest, a place of ancient magic. We must go there and call upon the magic of the forest to protect our people."

Elara's eyes shone with resolve. "Then let's go, Aiden. Together, we will protect our people and end this conflict once and for all."

The next morning, they set out on their journey, their hearts filled with determination and hope. The forest seemed to guide their steps, its ancient magic leading them towards their goal.

As they ventured deeper into the heart of Eldoria, the air grew thicker with enchantment, and the trees whispered secrets in a language only Elara could understand. They followed the path shown to them by the amulet, their hearts united in their quest to protect their people and end the threat of the witch hunters.

After hours of travel, they arrived at the hidden chamber. The entrance was concealed by a curtain of ivy, and the air was filled with a sense of ancient power. Aiden and Elara stepped inside, their hearts pounding with anticipation.

The chamber was a place of wonder and magic, its walls covered in ancient runes and symbols. In the center stood an altar, its surface smooth and polished. The air crackled with energy, and the ground seemed to pulse with the power of the forest.

Aiden and Elara approached the altar, their hands joined. They closed their eyes, focusing on the magic of the forest and the bond they shared. They began to chant, their voices resonating with the ancient power of the chamber.

"By the power of the ancients, we call upon the magic of the forest. Protect our people, end this conflict, and bring peace to Eldoria."

The air around them seemed to come alive, the magic of the forest swirling and coalescing around the altar. The ground trembled, and a surge of energy erupted from the chamber, spreading outwards in a wave of light and power.

As the magic surged through the forest, the witch hunters felt its force, their weapons rendered useless and their resolve shattered. The power of the forest overwhelmed them, neutralizing the threat they posed and ensuring the safety of the witches of Eldoria.

Aiden and Elara stood before the altar, their hearts filled with triumph and relief. They had done it. They had protected their people and ended the threat of the witch hunters. The bond they shared had given them the strength to overcome the challenges they faced, and their love had guided them to victory.

As they left the hidden chamber, the forest seemed to hum with life, its ancient magic restoring balance to the land. Aiden and Elara knew that their journey was far from over, but they faced the future with hope and determination, their hearts united in their quest for peace and harmony.

Together, they would continue to protect the enchanted forest of Eldoria, their love and magic a beacon of light in a world filled with darkness. And as they walked hand in hand through the forest, they knew that their bond would guide them through whatever challenges lay ahead, their hearts bound together by a love that was as powerful and enduring as the magic of the forest itself.

Chapter 5: The Love Spell

The Witch's Love Spell

THE AIR WAS THICK WITH tension as Aiden and Elara made their way through the forest, their hearts still heavy from the recent victory against the witch hunters. Despite their triumph, the knowledge of the royal decree and the ongoing danger to the witches of Eldoria loomed over them like a dark cloud. As they journeyed deeper into the forest, a plan began to form in Elara's mind, one born out of desperation and fear.

Elara knew that Aiden's loyalty was strong, but the ever-present threat of the kingdom's decree haunted her thoughts. She had seen the lengths to which the king and his knights would go to eradicate witches, and she couldn't shake the fear that Aiden might one day be forced to choose between her and his duty to Ravenspire. It was a fear that gnawed at her heart, and she was determined to find a way to secure his loyalty once and for all.

Elara's Decision: Casting the Love Spell

ONE EVENING, AS THEY set up camp near a serene glade, Elara's thoughts turned to a spell she had read about in one of her family's ancient grimoires—a love spell that could bind someone's heart to another's, ensuring unwavering loyalty and devotion. It was a powerful and risky spell, one that required great skill and a deep understanding of magic.

As she gathered herbs and prepared their evening meal, Elara's mind raced with the possibilities. The love she felt for Aiden was real, and she knew that his feelings for her were genuine. But the fear of losing him, of seeing him torn between his love for her and his duty to the kingdom, was too much to bear. She convinced herself that the spell would simply strengthen the bond they already shared, ensuring that nothing could come between them.

That night, as Aiden slept peacefully by the campfire, Elara took out her grimoire and began to prepare the ingredients for the spell. She whispered incantations under her breath, her hands moving with practiced precision as she mixed the herbs and magical elements required for the enchantment.

As she worked, doubt crept into her mind. Was this the right thing to do? Was she truly securing their love, or was she manipulating it? She pushed the doubts aside, focusing on her goal. She couldn't risk losing Aiden, not when their love had already faced so many challenges.

With the potion prepared, Elara approached Aiden and gently placed a few drops on his lips. She whispered the final incantation, feeling a surge of magic as the spell took effect. The air around them shimmered with an ethereal light, and Elara knew that the spell was complete.

She watched Aiden's peaceful face, her heart heavy with a mix of hope and guilt. She had done what she believed was necessary to protect their love, but she couldn't shake the nagging feeling that she had crossed a line. Only time would reveal the true consequences of her decision.

Consequences: Aiden's Behavior Changes

IN THE DAYS THAT FOLLOWED, Elara began to notice subtle changes in Aiden's behavior. He seemed more attentive, more protective, and his devotion to her grew stronger with each passing day. At first, Elara was relieved. The spell appeared to be working, and Aiden's loyalty was unwavering.

But as time went on, the changes became more pronounced. Aiden's protectiveness bordered on obsession, and he became increasingly possessive. He insisted on accompanying Elara everywhere, even on tasks that she had previously handled on her own. He watched her every move, his eyes filled with an intensity that both comforted and unnerved her.

One afternoon, as Elara gathered herbs near a stream, Aiden stood guard nearby, his eyes scanning the forest for any signs of danger. Elara couldn't help but notice the way his hand never left the hilt of his sword, his body tense and ready to spring into action at a moment's notice.

"Aiden, you don't need to be so on edge," Elara said gently, trying to ease his tension. "We're safe here."

Aiden's eyes softened as he looked at her. "I just want to make sure nothing happens to you, Elara. I couldn't bear to lose you."

Elara smiled, but the weight of her guilt pressed heavily on her heart. She had wanted to ensure Aiden's loyalty, but she hadn't anticipated the intensity of his devotion. It was as if the spell had amplified his feelings to an overwhelming degree, turning his love into an all-consuming obsession.

As the days turned into weeks, the changes in Aiden's behavior became more apparent to those around them. Other witches in the forest began to notice his constant presence at Elara's side, his unwavering attention and protectiveness. Whispers of concern and curiosity spread through the community, but Elara brushed them aside, insisting that everything was fine.

Moral Quandary: Regret and Fear

DESPITE HER ATTEMPTS to maintain a sense of normalcy, Elara couldn't ignore the growing unease in her heart. She had wanted to protect their love, but now she feared that she had manipulated it beyond recognition. The bond they shared was real, but the spell had twisted it into something more intense and consuming.

One evening, as they sat by the campfire, Elara's thoughts weighed heavily on her mind. She watched Aiden as he tended to the fire, his every movement filled with a sense of purpose and devotion. She knew that she needed to confront the consequences of her actions, but the fear of what she might find held her back.

"Aiden," she began hesitantly, her voice trembling slightly, "there's something I need to talk to you about."

Aiden looked up, his eyes filled with concern. "What is it, Elara?"

Elara took a deep breath, her heart pounding in her chest. "Do you ever feel like your feelings for me have changed? That they've become... stronger than they were before?"

Aiden's brow furrowed in confusion. "I love you, Elara. I've always loved you. Why do you ask?"

Elara bit her lip, struggling to find the right words. "I just... I wonder if something might have influenced your feelings. If there's a reason why you're so protective of me now."

Aiden's expression softened, and he reached out to take her hand. "Elara, my feelings for you are real. I would do anything to protect you, to keep you safe. That's how much you mean to me."

Elara's heart ached at his words. She wanted to believe him, to trust in the love they shared. But the nagging guilt in her heart wouldn't let her rest. She had to know the truth, to understand the full extent of the consequences of her actions.

As the days passed, Elara's internal struggle grew more intense. She couldn't shake the feeling that she had betrayed Aiden's trust, that she had manipulated the love they shared. The weight of her guilt pressed down on her, making it difficult to focus on anything else.

One night, unable to bear the burden any longer, Elara sought out the counsel of an elder witch named Isolde. Isolde was wise and experienced, known for her deep understanding of magic and the human heart. If anyone could help Elara navigate her moral quandary, it was her.

Elara found Isolde in a secluded grove, tending to her garden of rare and magical herbs. The elder witch looked up as Elara approached, her eyes filled with warmth and understanding.

"Elara, my dear," Isolde said gently, "what troubles you?"

Elara hesitated, unsure of how to begin. But the kind look in Isolde's eyes gave her the courage to speak. She poured out her heart, confessing her fears and regrets, the spell she had cast, and the changes she had noticed in Aiden's behavior.

Isolde listened patiently, her expression thoughtful as she took in Elara's words. When Elara finished, she placed a comforting hand on her shoulder.

"Magic is a powerful force, Elara," Isolde said softly. "It can shape our world and influence our hearts. But it is also a force that must be wielded with care and respect. The spell you cast may have had unintended consequences, amplifying Aiden's feelings to an unnatural degree."

Elara's eyes filled with tears. "I didn't mean to manipulate him, Isolde. I just wanted to protect our love, to ensure his loyalty."

Isolde nodded. "I understand your intentions, my dear. But love cannot be forced or manipulated. It must be allowed to grow and flourish naturally. The spell may have altered Aiden's feelings, but the love you share is still real. You must find a way to restore the balance, to honor the true nature of your bond."

Elara's heart ached with regret, but Isolde's words gave her a glimmer of hope. She knew that she needed to take responsibility for her actions and find a way to undo the spell. It would not be easy, but she was determined to make things right.

Undoing the Spell: Seeking Redemption

WITH ISOLDE'S GUIDANCE, Elara set out to find a way to reverse the spell. She delved into her grimoire, seeking out ancient texts and incantations that might hold the key to restoring the natural balance of their love. The process was arduous and filled with uncertainty, but Elara's resolve never wavered.

As she worked, Aiden remained by her side, his devotion unwavering. He sensed the turmoil in Elara's heart and did everything he could to support her, even as his own feelings of protectiveness and obsession grew stronger.

One evening, as Elara pored over her grimoire by the light of the campfire, she found a passage that spoke of a ritual to cleanse and purify a bond altered by magic. It was a complex and delicate process, requiring a deep connection between the two individuals and a willingness to face the truth of their feelings.

Elara knew that this was the answer she had been seeking. She called Aiden to her side, her heart filled with a mix of hope and fear.

"Aiden," she said softly, "I've found a way to restore the balance in our bond. But it will require us to face the truth of our feelings and to trust in the love we share."

Aiden's eyes were filled with determination. "I trust you, Elara. Whatever it takes, I'm with you."

With Aiden's support, Elara prepared for the ritual. She gathered the necessary ingredients and inscribed the sacred symbols on the ground. The air around them hummed with magic as they stood before the altar, their hands joined and their hearts united.

Elara began to chant, her voice resonating with the ancient power of the ritual. The symbols on the ground glowed with a soft, ethereal light, and a surge of energy enveloped them. As the ritual progressed, Elara felt the weight of the spell begin to lift, the unnatural intensity of Aiden's feelings easing away.

Aiden closed his eyes, his mind and heart open to the cleansing power of the ritual. He felt a sense of clarity and calm wash over him, the obsessive protectiveness giving way to a deeper, more genuine love.

When the ritual was complete, the light around them faded, and Elara and Aiden stood in the quiet stillness of the forest. They looked at each other, their eyes filled with the truth of their feelings.

"Elara," Aiden said softly, "I love you. Truly and deeply. I'm sorry if my actions ever caused you pain or fear."

Elara's eyes filled with tears, and she reached out to touch his face. "I love you too, Aiden. And I'm sorry for any harm I may have caused. Our love is real, and I want to honor it for what it truly is."

They embraced, their hearts filled with a sense of peace and redemption. The spell had been undone, and their bond had been restored to its natural state. They knew that their love would continue to face challenges, but they were ready to face them together, with honesty and trust.

Moving Forward: A New Beginning

WITH THE SPELL BEHIND them, Aiden and Elara continued their journey, their hearts lighter and their bond stronger than ever. They faced each challenge with renewed determination, drawing strength from their love and their commitment to each other.

As they traveled through the enchanted forest, they encountered other witches who had been affected by the royal decree. Aiden used his knowledge and skills to help them find safety, while Elara worked to heal the wounds left by the conflict.

Their efforts did not go unnoticed. The witches of Eldoria began to see Aiden not as an enemy, but as an ally and protector. His bravery and dedication earned him their respect and gratitude, and he became a symbol of hope and unity.

One day, as they rested by a tranquil lake, Aiden took Elara's hand and looked into her eyes. "Elara, we've been through so much together. Our love has faced trials and challenges, but it has only grown stronger. I want to spend the rest of my life with you, facing whatever comes our way."

Elara's heart swelled with love and joy. "Aiden, I feel the same. Our journey is just beginning, and I want to walk it with you by my side."

With their hearts united, Aiden and Elara pledged to continue their quest to protect the enchanted forest and its inhabitants. They knew that their love was a powerful force, one that could overcome any obstacle and bring light to the darkest of times.

As they walked hand in hand through the forest, the trees whispered their blessings, and the magic of Eldoria embraced them. They were ready to face whatever challenges lay ahead, secure in the knowledge that their love was true and unwavering.

Together, they would forge a future filled with hope, love, and magic, their hearts bound by a bond that was as powerful and enduring as the enchanted forest itself.

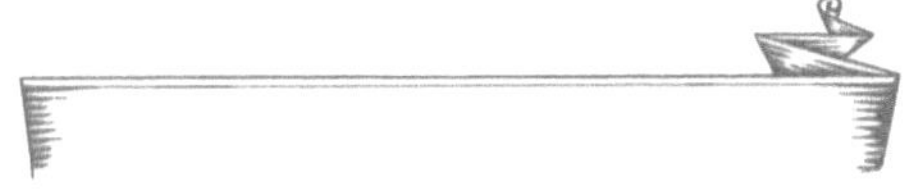

Chapter 6: The Discovery

The Witch's Love Spell

THE DAYS AFTER THE ritual were some of the happiest Aiden and Elara had known. Their bond, purified and renewed, gave them strength and solace. They continued their efforts to protect the enchanted forest of Eldoria, working together with other witches and creatures to restore balance and peace. The royal decree still loomed over them, but their love gave them the courage to face whatever dangers came their way.

One sunny afternoon, they returned to Elara's cottage to rest and replenish their supplies. The cottage, nestled in a serene glade, was a sanctuary away from the troubles that plagued the outside world. The air was filled with the scent of blooming flowers, and birds sang melodies that soothed their weary souls.

As Elara busied herself with brewing potions and tending to her garden, Aiden explored the cottage, admiring the various artifacts and books that adorned the shelves. His eyes fell on a particularly old and weathered book, its cover adorned with symbols and runes he did not recognize. Curious, he picked it up and began to leaf through its pages.

Truth Unveiled: Aiden Finds Out About the Love Spell

AS AIDEN READ THE ANCIENT text, he came across a passage that caught his attention. The description of a love spell, one that bound a person's heart and mind to another's, seemed all too familiar. His heart pounded as he continued reading, the details matching the changes he had experienced in his own feelings.

He realized with a growing sense of dread that the spell described was the same one Elara had cast on him. The intensity of his protectiveness, the overwhelming devotion—everything suddenly made sense. Aiden felt a cold wave of betrayal wash over him as he absorbed the implications of what he had discovered.

His mind raced with conflicting emotions. The love he felt for Elara was real, but it had been manipulated by the spell. He thought back to their conversations, the moments of doubt and the ritual they had performed to cleanse their bond. Had it all been a lie?

Elara entered the room, her smile fading as she saw the book in Aiden's hands and the look of shock and betrayal on his face. "Aiden, what is it?" she asked, her voice trembling.

Aiden's hands shook as he held up the book. "This," he said, his voice cold, "is this what you did to me? Did you cast a spell on me to make me love you?"

Elara's heart sank, and she felt a surge of guilt and fear. She knew that this moment would come, that the truth would eventually be revealed. But facing it now, seeing the pain in Aiden's eyes, was almost unbearable.

"Aiden, I..." she began, her voice breaking, "I can explain. I did cast the spell, but it was never to make you love me. I just wanted to ensure your loyalty, to protect what we had. I was afraid of losing you."

Aiden's eyes flashed with anger and hurt. "You manipulated my feelings, Elara. You took away my free will. How can I trust anything we had after this?"

Betrayal: Aiden Distances Himself from Elara

UNABLE TO BEAR THE weight of his emotions, Aiden turned and left the cottage, his heart heavy with betrayal and confusion. He needed time to process what he had learned, to understand the full extent of Elara's actions. The love he felt for her was now tainted by the knowledge that it had been influenced by magic.

Elara watched him go, her heart breaking with each step he took away from her. She knew that she had made a terrible mistake, and the consequences of her actions were now unfolding before her eyes. She felt a deep sense of guilt and sorrow, knowing that she had betrayed the trust of the man she loved.

Days turned into weeks, and Aiden kept his distance from Elara. He threw himself into his duties, helping the witches of Eldoria and working to protect the forest. But the pain of betrayal lingered, a constant reminder of the trust that had been shattered.

Elara, tormented by her guilt, sought solace in her magic and her studies. She spent countless hours poring over her grimoires, searching for a way to reverse the spell and make amends for her actions. The weight of her guilt was a heavy burden, and she knew that she needed to find a way to make things right.

Elara's Guilt: Seeking Redemption

ELARA'S DAYS WERE FILLED with a relentless pursuit of redemption. She delved into the deepest recesses of her magical knowledge, seeking a way to undo the spell and restore the natural balance of their love. She consulted with elder witches, sought guidance from ancient spirits, and performed countless rituals in her quest for a solution.

One evening, as she sat by the campfire, her heart heavy with despair, Isolde approached her. The elder witch had been a source of wisdom and comfort throughout Elara's journey, and her presence now was a beacon of hope in the darkness.

"Elara," Isolde said gently, "I can see the pain and guilt you carry. But you must remember that magic is not inherently good or evil. It is the intent behind it that shapes its outcome. You made a mistake, but you also have the power to make things right."

Elara looked up, her eyes filled with tears. "I don't know how to undo the harm I've caused, Isolde. I've searched for a way to reverse the spell, but nothing seems to work."

Isolde placed a comforting hand on her shoulder. "Sometimes, the answer lies not in the magic itself, but in the heart. You must confront Aiden, speak your truth, and seek his forgiveness. Only then can the true healing begin."

Elara nodded, knowing that Isolde was right. She needed to face Aiden, to confess her actions and seek his forgiveness. It was the only way to restore the trust that had been broken and to heal the wounds that had been inflicted.

Confrontation and Confession

DETERMINED TO MAKE amends, Elara set out to find Aiden. She knew that he had been working tirelessly to protect the witches of Eldoria, and she hoped that he would be willing to listen to her. Her heart was filled with a mix of hope and fear as she approached the place where she knew he would be.

Aiden was deep in conversation with a group of witches when he saw Elara approaching. His expression hardened, and he excused himself from the group, walking towards her with a guarded look in his eyes.

"Elara," he said, his voice cold and distant, "what do you want?"

Elara took a deep breath, her heart pounding. "Aiden, I need to talk to you. Please, just hear me out."

Aiden crossed his arms, his gaze unwavering. "I'm listening."

Elara's voice trembled as she began to speak. "I know that I hurt you, and I know that I betrayed your trust. Casting that spell was a mistake, one born out of fear and desperation. I thought I was protecting our love, but I see now that I was wrong. I took away your free will, and for that, I am truly sorry."

Aiden's expression softened slightly, but his eyes remained wary. "Why did you do it, Elara? Why didn't you trust in what we had?"

Elara's eyes filled with tears. "I was afraid, Aiden. Afraid of losing you, afraid of the royal decree, afraid of the dangers that surrounded us. I thought that by casting the spell, I could ensure your loyalty and protect what we had. But I see now that I was wrong. I let my fear cloud my judgment, and I hurt you in the process."

Aiden's heart ached at the pain in Elara's voice. He could see the genuine remorse in her eyes, the weight of her guilt and sorrow. But the betrayal still lingered, a wound that had yet to heal.

"Elara," he said softly, "I want to believe you. I want to trust you again. But it's not that simple. The spell changed everything, and I need time to process what happened."

Elara nodded, her heart heavy with understanding. "I know, Aiden. And I will do whatever it takes to make things right. I will find a way to reverse the spell, to restore the natural balance of our love. I just need you to know that I am truly sorry, and I will never stop trying to earn your forgiveness."

Aiden looked into her eyes, seeing the sincerity and determination that had always drawn him to her. He knew that the road to healing would be long and difficult, but he also knew that their love was worth fighting for.

"Thank you, Elara," he said softly. "I need time, but I promise that I will try to move past this. I want to find a way to heal, for both of us."

Elara's heart swelled with a mix of hope and relief. She knew that the journey ahead would be challenging, but she was determined to make things right. With Aiden's willingness to forgive, she felt a renewed sense of purpose and resolve.

The Path to Redemption

IN THE DAYS THAT FOLLOWED, Elara continued her efforts to find a way to reverse the spell. She sought guidance from Isolde and other elder witches, learning new incantations and rituals that might help restore the natural balance of their love. She also worked tirelessly to support the witches of Eldoria, using her magic to heal and protect those in need.

Aiden, meanwhile, focused on his duties as a knight, but he could not escape the thoughts of Elara and the love they had shared. He found himself thinking about her often, the memories of their time together mingling with the pain of betrayal. He knew that he needed to find a way to move forward, to heal the wounds that had been inflicted.

One evening, as the sun set over the enchanted forest, Aiden found himself drawn to the hidden cave where he and Elara had performed the ritual to cleanse their bond. The cave held a special significance for him, a place where they had faced their fears and strengthened their love.

As he stood in the quiet stillness of the cave, Aiden closed his eyes and allowed himself to feel the full weight of his emotions. He thought about the love he had for Elara, the trust that had been shattered, and the hope for redemption. He knew that healing would take time, but he also knew that he was willing to try.

A New Ritual: Restoring Balance

WITH RENEWED DETERMINATION, Aiden sought out Elara. He found her in the secluded grove where Isolde often conducted her rituals, her expression one of deep concentration as she worked with the elder witch.

"Elara," Aiden said softly, his voice carrying a note of hope, "I think I'm ready to try to heal our bond. I want to move forward, to find a way to restore the trust that was broken."

Elara's eyes filled with a mix of surprise and relief. "Aiden, I'm so glad to hear that. I've been working with Isolde to find a way to reverse the spell and restore the natural balance of our love."

Isolde nodded, her eyes filled with wisdom and understanding. "There is a ritual we can perform, one that requires both of you to be fully open and honest with each other. It will cleanse the remnants of the spell and allow your bond to heal naturally."

Aiden and Elara exchanged a look of determination, knowing that this was the path they needed to take. Together, they followed Isolde's guidance, preparing for the ritual that would help them find redemption and restore their love.

The night of the ritual was one of quiet anticipation. The grove was bathed in the soft light of the full moon, and the air was filled with the scent of blooming flowers and the gentle rustle of leaves. Isolde guided Aiden and Elara through the steps of the ritual, her voice a soothing presence as they prepared to cleanse their bond.

They stood before a stone altar, their hands joined and their hearts open. Isolde began to chant, her voice resonating with the ancient magic of the forest. Aiden and Elara closed their eyes, allowing the energy of the ritual to envelop them.

As the ritual progressed, they spoke their truths, their voices filled with the weight of their emotions. Aiden spoke of his love for Elara, the pain of betrayal, and his hope for healing. Elara confessed her guilt and sorrow, her determination to make things right and her unwavering love for Aiden.

The air around them shimmered with a soft, ethereal light, and the symbols on the ground glowed with the power of the ritual. They felt a surge of energy, a cleansing force that washed away the remnants of the spell and restored the natural balance of their bond.

When the ritual was complete, Aiden and Elara stood in the quiet stillness of the grove, their hearts filled with a sense of peace and renewal. They looked into each other's eyes, seeing the truth of their feelings reflected back at them.

"Elara," Aiden said softly, his voice filled with emotion, "I forgive you. I know that our love is real, and I want to move forward together."

Tears of relief and joy filled Elara's eyes. "Thank you, Aiden. I promise to honor the true nature of our bond, to love and trust you with all my heart."

They embraced, their hearts united in a renewed commitment to each other and to the love they shared. The road to healing had been long and difficult, but they had found their way back to each other, stronger and more determined than ever.

Moving Forward: A Future Filled with Hope

WITH THE RITUAL BEHIND them, Aiden and Elara faced the future with hope and determination. They continued their efforts to protect the enchanted forest and its inhabitants, working together to heal the wounds left by the royal decree and the conflict that had followed.

Their bond, now free from the influence of the spell, was stronger and more genuine than ever. They faced each challenge with a renewed sense of purpose, drawing strength from the love they shared and the trust they had rebuilt.

The witches of Eldoria looked to Aiden and Elara as symbols of hope and unity, their love a testament to the power of forgiveness and redemption. Together, they worked to create a future where witches and humans could coexist in harmony, their hearts united in a common goal.

One evening, as they sat by the campfire, Aiden took Elara's hand and looked into her eyes. "Elara, we've been through so much together. Our love has faced trials and challenges, but it has only grown stronger. I want to spend the rest of my life with you, facing whatever comes our way."

Elara's heart swelled with love and joy. "Aiden, I feel the same. Our journey is just beginning, and I want to walk it with you by my side."

With their hearts united, Aiden and Elara pledged to continue their quest to protect the enchanted forest and its inhabitants. They knew that their love was a powerful force, one that could overcome any obstacle and bring light to the darkest of times.

As they walked hand in hand through the forest, the trees whispered their blessings, and the magic of Eldoria embraced them. They were ready to face whatever challenges lay ahead, secure in the knowledge that their love was true and unwavering.

Together, they would forge a future filled with hope, love, and magic, their hearts bound by a bond that was as powerful and enduring as the enchanted forest itself.

Chapter 7: The Dark Sorcerer

The Witch's Love Spell

The tranquil beauty of Eldoria had been restored, but the peace was fleeting. In the depths of the enchanted forest, an ominous presence began to stir, casting a dark shadow over both Eldoria and the kingdom of Ravenspire. The air grew thick with tension, and the creatures of the forest became restless, sensing the return of an ancient evil.

Introduction of Antagonist: The Dark Sorcerer

FAR BEYOND THE REACH of the sun's light, deep within the dark heart of Eldoria, a powerful dark sorcerer named Malakar had awakened from his centuries-long slumber. Malakar, a master of dark magic and a formidable foe, had once been the scourge of both Eldoria and Ravenspire. His hunger for power and domination had led to a reign of terror, leaving destruction in his wake.

Sealed away by the combined efforts of witches and knights, Malakar had remained dormant, trapped in a prison of enchanted stone. But now, the seals had weakened, and his dark magic had grown strong enough to break free. His eyes, glowing with malevolent intent, scanned the forest as he emerged from his prison, his mind already plotting his return to power.

Malakar's first act was to summon his loyal minions, creatures of darkness and shadows that had once served him. They answered his call, materializing from the depths of the forest to pledge their allegiance once more. With his army assembled, Malakar set his sights on reclaiming Eldoria and Ravenspire, determined to bend both realms to his will.

New Mission: Aiden and Elara Must Stop the Sorcerer

NEWS OF MALAKAR'S RETURN spread quickly through Eldoria and Ravenspire, sowing fear and panic among the inhabitants. The elders of Eldoria convened an emergency council, seeking a way to combat the rising threat. Elara, known for her strength and wisdom, was summoned to the council to offer her insights and leadership.

At the same time, the knights of Ravenspire received word of Malakar's resurgence. King Alden, recognizing the gravity of the situation, called upon his most trusted knights to form a task force to confront the dark sorcerer. Among those summoned was Aiden, whose loyalty and bravery had earned him the king's trust.

As fate would have it, the paths of Aiden and Elara were destined to cross once more. The council of Eldoria and the knights of Ravenspire agreed to a joint effort, recognizing that only by working together could they hope to defeat Malakar and protect their realms.

Aiden arrived at the council meeting, his heart heavy with the knowledge that he would once again be working alongside Elara. Their relationship, strained by the betrayal of the love spell, had only recently begun to heal. The thought of facing a new and deadly threat together filled him with a mix of determination and uncertainty.

Elara, too, felt the weight of their history as she prepared for the mission. She knew that their bond had been tested and strained, but she also recognized the importance of their partnership. The fate of Eldoria and Ravenspire depended on their ability to work together.

Reluctant Partnership: Working Together Despite Strained Relationship

THE COUNCIL MEETING was tense as the leaders of Eldoria and Ravenspire outlined their plan. Aiden and Elara stood side by side, their expressions serious as they listened to the details of the mission. The plan was to locate Malakar's lair, disrupt his dark rituals, and defeat him before his power could grow any stronger.

"Aiden, Elara," one of the elder witches said, addressing them directly, "you two have proven yourselves capable and resourceful. We need you to lead this mission. Your combined strengths and knowledge are our best hope of defeating Malakar."

Aiden nodded, his jaw set with determination. "We will do whatever it takes to protect our homes and our people."

Elara glanced at Aiden, her eyes filled with resolve. "Yes, we will. But we must be prepared for the challenges ahead. Malakar is a formidable foe, and his dark magic is powerful."

The leaders continued to discuss their strategy, and it was clear that Aiden and Elara would need to put aside their personal feelings to focus on the mission. They exchanged a look of mutual understanding, knowing that their past could not be allowed to interfere with their duty.

As the meeting concluded, Aiden and Elara found themselves alone, the weight of their partnership pressing down on them. Aiden broke the silence, his voice steady but strained.

"Elara, I know we have a difficult history, but we need to work together. Our realms depend on it."

Elara nodded, her expression earnest. "I agree, Aiden. I want to put the past behind us and focus on the task at hand. We must be united if we are to defeat Malakar."

Aiden took a deep breath, feeling a sense of relief at her words. "Thank you, Elara. Let's do this."

The Journey to Malakar's Lair

THE JOURNEY TO MALAKAR'S lair was fraught with danger and uncertainty. Aiden and Elara, accompanied by a select group of witches and knights, made their way through the dense forest, their senses alert for any signs of the dark sorcerer's presence. The air grew colder and more oppressive as they ventured deeper into the heart of Eldoria, the trees casting long shadows that seemed to reach out and grasp at them.

Despite the tension between them, Aiden and Elara worked together seamlessly, their combined skills and knowledge proving invaluable. Aiden's combat prowess and tactical acumen complemented Elara's magical abilities and deep understanding of the forest. They communicated effectively, their past differences set aside in the face of the greater threat.

As they traveled, they encountered numerous obstacles, from treacherous terrain to hostile creatures summoned by Malakar's dark magic. Each challenge tested their resolve and their ability to work as a team, but they pressed on, driven by their shared determination to protect their realms.

One evening, as they set up camp near a small clearing, Aiden and Elara found themselves alone, the rest of the group busy with preparations. The silence between them was heavy, filled with unspoken words and unresolved emotions.

Aiden finally broke the silence, his voice quiet but firm. "Elara, I want you to know that I appreciate your dedication to this mission. I know it's not easy, given everything we've been through."

Elara looked at him, her eyes reflecting the complexity of her feelings. "Thank you, Aiden. I know I've made mistakes, but I want to make things right. Our love is real, and I believe in us. But right now, we need to focus on defeating Malakar."

Aiden nodded, a sense of understanding passing between them. "I believe in us too, Elara. Let's get through this together."

Facing Malakar

AS THEY APPROACHED Malakar's lair, the air grew thick with dark magic, and the forest itself seemed to writhe in pain. The ground was littered with twisted roots and decaying vegetation, a stark contrast to the vibrant beauty that once defined Eldoria. A sense of foreboding hung over the group as they prepared for the final confrontation.

Malakar's lair was a cavernous structure carved into the side of a mountain, its entrance guarded by grotesque statues and enchanted barriers. The group paused at the entrance, their resolve tested by the malevolent energy emanating from within.

Aiden turned to the group, his expression resolute. "This is it. We need to stay focused and work together. Malakar is powerful, but we can defeat him if we stand united."

Elara stepped forward, her hands glowing with a soft, green light. "I'll take down the barriers. Be ready to move in as soon as they're down."

With a series of precise incantations, Elara shattered the enchanted barriers, clearing the way for the group to enter the lair. They moved swiftly and silently, their senses heightened as they navigated the dark corridors.

As they ventured deeper into the lair, they encountered Malakar's minions—shadowy creatures that lurked in the darkness, ready to attack. Aiden and the knights fought valiantly, their swords gleaming in the dim light as they cut down their foes. Elara and the witches provided magical support, casting spells to weaken and disorient the creatures.

The battles were fierce and relentless, but the group pressed on, driven by their determination to reach Malakar and end his reign of terror. Finally, they entered a vast chamber, its walls lined with ancient runes and sigils that pulsed with dark energy.

At the center of the chamber stood Malakar, his presence commanding and terrifying. His eyes glowed with malevolent intent as he surveyed the intruders, a sinister smile curling across his lips.

"Welcome," Malakar hissed, his voice echoing through the chamber. "You are brave to come here, but your efforts are futile. I will crush you, and both Eldoria and Ravenspire will fall under my rule."

Aiden stepped forward, his sword raised defiantly. "We will never let that happen, Malakar. Your reign of terror ends here."

Elara joined him, her hands crackling with magical energy. "We will fight for our homes, our people, and for the light that still shines in this world."

Malakar laughed, a chilling sound that sent shivers down their spines. "Very well. Let us see if your courage matches your words."

The Battle Against Malakar

THE BATTLE THAT ENSUED was one of epic proportions, a clash of light and darkness that shook the very foundations of the lair. Aiden and Elara fought side by side, their movements synchronized and their hearts united in their determination to defeat Malakar.

Aiden's sword glowed with a brilliant light, each strike infused with the power of the enchanted amulet around his neck. He moved with precision and strength, parrying Malakar's dark magic and countering with powerful blows.

Elara's magic was a force to be reckoned with, her spells weaving through the air with a grace and intensity that left their enemies reeling. She summoned elemental forces, conjuring flames and lightning to strike at Malakar and his minions.

The other knights and witches joined the fray, their combined efforts creating a formidable force that pushed Malakar to his limits. The chamber was filled with the sounds of clashing steel and crackling magic, the air thick with the scent of ozone and the acrid tang of dark energy.

Despite their best efforts, Malakar proved to be a formidable opponent. His dark magic was powerful and relentless, and he seemed to draw strength from the very shadows that surrounded him. He unleashed waves of dark energy, forcing Aiden and Elara to fight with every ounce of their strength and skill.

Aiden felt the strain of the battle weighing on him, but he refused to give in. He glanced at Elara, her face set with determination, and drew strength from the bond they shared. Together, they could overcome any obstacle.

With a surge of resolve, Aiden pressed forward, his sword blazing with light as he launched a fierce assault on Malakar. Elara joined him, her magic intertwining with his attacks to create a devastating combination of light and power.

Malakar snarled in frustration, his defenses weakening under the relentless onslaught. Aiden and Elara pressed their advantage, their hearts and minds united in their goal.

Finally, with a powerful strike, Aiden's sword pierced Malakar's defenses, the blade sinking deep into the dark sorcerer's chest. Malakar let out a scream of rage and pain, his body convulsing as the light of the enchanted amulet overwhelmed his dark magic.

Elara raised her hands, casting a final incantation that channeled the combined power of the group into a concentrated blast of light. The chamber was filled with a blinding radiance, and Malakar's form disintegrated, his dark essence consumed by the light.

As the light faded, the chamber grew quiet, the oppressive darkness lifting to reveal the weary but triumphant faces of the group. Aiden and Elara stood together, their hearts filled with relief and gratitude.

Aftermath and Reflection

THE DEFEAT OF MALAKAR marked a turning point for both Eldoria and Ravenspire. The dark sorcerer's reign of terror had been ended, and the threat to their homes and people had been vanquished. The group made their way back to the surface, their spirits lifted by the knowledge that they had achieved what had once seemed impossible.

Aiden and Elara found themselves standing together in the heart of the forest, the gentle breeze carrying the scent of blooming flowers and the promise of a new beginning. They looked at each other, their eyes filled with a deep sense of understanding and connection.

"Aiden," Elara said softly, "I know that our journey has been filled with challenges and mistakes, but I am grateful for the strength and love we have found together."

Aiden took her hand, his heart swelling with love and pride. "Elara, our bond has been tested, but it has only made us stronger. I am proud to stand by your side, now and always."

As they walked hand in hand through the forest, the trees whispered their blessings, and the magic of Eldoria embraced them. They were ready to face whatever challenges lay ahead, secure in the knowledge that their love was true and unwavering.

Together, they would forge a future filled with hope, love, and magic, their hearts bound by a bond that was as powerful and enduring as the enchanted forest itself.

The Road Ahead

THE DEFEAT OF MALAKAR was a significant victory, but Aiden and Elara knew that their work was far from over. The wounds left by the conflict needed time to heal, and the trust between Eldoria and Ravenspire had to be rebuilt.

They returned to their respective homes, carrying with them the lessons they had learned and the strength they had gained. Aiden continued to serve as a knight, using his experiences to promote understanding and cooperation between humans and witches. Elara dedicated herself to healing the land and her people, her magic a beacon of hope and renewal.

Their paths continued to intersect, their love a constant source of inspiration and resilience. They faced new challenges with the same determination and unity that had carried them through the battle against Malakar, their hearts steadfast in their commitment to each other and to the protection of their realms.

As the years passed, Aiden and Elara's bond grew deeper, their love a testament to the power of forgiveness and the strength of the human spirit. They became symbols of hope and unity, their story a legend that would be told for generations to come.

And so, the enchanted forest of Eldoria flourished, its magic intertwined with the love and courage of those who called it home. Aiden and Elara's journey was far from over, but they faced the future with hope and determination, their hearts united in a bond that would endure for all time.

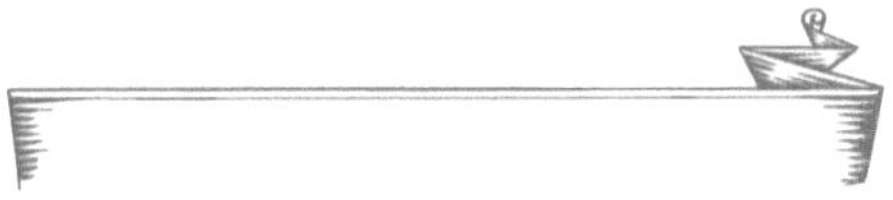

Chapter 8: The Journey Begins

The Witch's Love Spell

The dawn broke over Eldoria, painting the sky with hues of pink and gold as the first light of morning pierced through the dense canopy of trees. The forest, alive with the sounds of waking birds and rustling leaves, seemed to hold its breath in anticipation of the journey that lay ahead. Aiden and Elara stood side by side, their hearts heavy with the knowledge of the perilous quest they were about to undertake. The dark sorcerer Malakar, though defeated, had left behind traces of his dark magic that threatened the delicate balance of their world.

Adventure: Embarking on the Journey

AIDEN ADJUSTED THE straps of his armor, the polished metal glinting in the morning light. He turned to Elara, who was securing her pack and checking the contents of her satchel, filled with potions and magical artifacts. Her eyes, usually so filled with warmth and understanding, were now focused and determined.

"Are you ready?" Aiden asked, his voice steady despite the undercurrent of tension.

Elara nodded, her gaze meeting his. "As ready as I'll ever be. This journey will not be easy, but we have faced great challenges before. We can do this, Aiden."

Aiden offered a reassuring smile, though his heart was heavy with the memories of their past struggles. "We'll find Malakar's lair and put an end to his dark magic. Together."

With a final nod, they set off, their steps guided by a shared sense of purpose. The path before them was shrouded in mist, the air cool and crisp. The forest, once a place of refuge and serenity, now seemed to teem with unseen dangers. Aiden and Elara moved cautiously, their senses heightened and their minds alert to any signs of trouble.

Obstacles: Facing Magical Creatures and Challenges

THEIR JOURNEY TOOK them through dense thickets and along winding paths, the landscape changing as they ventured deeper into the heart of Eldoria. The forest was alive with magic, its ancient trees and hidden glades holding secrets both wondrous and perilous. As they traveled, they encountered various magical creatures, each posing its own unique challenge.

One afternoon, as they made their way through a particularly dense part of the forest, they heard a series of low growls and rustling leaves. Aiden drew his sword, and Elara prepared a defensive spell, their eyes scanning the underbrush for the source of the sound.

Suddenly, a pack of shadow wolves emerged from the trees, their eyes glowing with an unnatural light. These creatures, twisted by Malakar's dark magic, were both ferocious and relentless. Aiden and Elara moved in tandem, their movements synchronized as they fought off the wolves. Aiden's sword flashed in the dappled light, each strike precise and powerful. Elara's spells crackled with energy, creating barriers and blasting the wolves with bursts of light.

Despite their combined efforts, the wolves were relentless. They circled around, their growls filling the air with a sense of impending doom. Aiden and Elara were pushed back, their breaths coming in heavy gasps as they struggled to keep the creatures at bay.

"We need to find a way to drive them off," Elara called out, her voice strained with effort.

Aiden nodded, his mind racing for a solution. He glanced at the enchanted amulet around his neck, feeling its protective energy pulsing against his skin. "The amulet," he said, his voice filled with sudden realization. "Its magic might be able to dispel the darkness that's controlling them."

Elara's eyes widened with understanding. "It's worth a try. Focus the amulet's energy, and I'll cast a spell to amplify it."

With a determined nod, Aiden held the amulet aloft, its light growing brighter as he channeled its magic. Elara raised her hands, chanting an incantation that wove their energies together. The amulet's light intensified, spreading out in a brilliant wave that enveloped the shadow wolves.

The creatures yelped and howled, their forms dissolving into wisps of darkness as the light purged the dark magic from their bodies. Within moments, the clearing was quiet once more, the air filled with the lingering glow of the amulet's light.

Aiden and Elara stood together, their hearts pounding from the exertion and the intensity of the battle. They exchanged a look of relief and mutual respect, their bond strengthened by the victory they had achieved together.

"Well done," Aiden said, his voice filled with admiration. "We make a good team."

Elara smiled, her eyes sparkling with a mix of pride and affection. "We always have, Aiden. No matter what challenges we face, we can overcome them together."

Healing Wounds: Reconciling and Understanding Each Other's Perspectives

AS THEY CONTINUED THEIR journey, the challenges they faced served to bring Aiden and Elara closer together. Each battle, each obstacle, was a reminder of the strength they found in their partnership. Despite the lingering tension from their past conflicts, they began to open up to each other, sharing their thoughts and feelings in a way that helped to heal the wounds between them.

One evening, as they set up camp near a tranquil stream, Aiden and Elara sat by the fire, the warmth and light creating a comforting cocoon around them. The day's journey had been arduous, and the quiet moment offered a chance for reflection.

"Aiden," Elara began, her voice soft and contemplative, "I've been thinking a lot about everything that's happened between us. The mistakes I've made, the trust that was broken... I want you to know how deeply sorry I am."

Aiden looked at her, his expression thoughtful. "Elara, I know you regret what happened. And I understand why you did it. Fear and love can make us do things we never thought we would. But what matters now is that we've moved past it and we're working together."

Elara nodded, her eyes filled with gratitude. "I still worry, though. I worry that the darkness we've faced has left scars that we might never fully heal from."

Aiden reached out, taking her hand in his. "We all carry scars, Elara. But it's how we move forward that defines us. I believe in our love, and I believe that we can overcome anything as long as we're together."

Elara's heart swelled with emotion, and she squeezed his hand. "Thank you, Aiden. Your faith in us means everything to me."

As the night deepened, they continued to talk, their conversations flowing freely and honestly. They spoke of their hopes and fears, their dreams for the future, and the strength they found in each other. With each word, they felt the wounds between them begin to heal, their bond growing stronger and more resilient.

Deeper into the Forest

THE FOLLOWING DAYS were filled with a renewed sense of purpose and unity. Aiden and Elara faced each challenge with unwavering determination, their partnership a beacon of hope in the midst of darkness. They encountered various magical creatures, each battle testing their resolve and strengthening their bond.

One afternoon, they came across a treacherous ravine, its depths shrouded in mist. The only way across was a narrow, rickety bridge that swayed precariously in the wind. Aiden stepped forward, his eyes scanning the bridge for any signs of weakness.

"We need to be careful," he said, his voice serious. "This bridge doesn't look stable."

Elara nodded, her eyes narrowing with determination. "We'll take it one step at a time. I'll use my magic to reinforce the bridge as we go."

With a shared look of resolve, they began to cross the bridge, their movements slow and deliberate. Elara focused her magic, weaving it into the structure of the bridge to strengthen it and prevent it from collapsing. Aiden led the way, his eyes constantly scanning for any signs of danger.

Halfway across, the bridge creaked ominously, and a section of the planks gave way beneath Aiden's feet. He grabbed onto the ropes, his heart racing as he dangled over the abyss.

"Hold on, Aiden!" Elara called out, her voice filled with urgency. She focused her magic, reinforcing the ropes and creating a platform beneath him.

With her help, Aiden pulled himself back onto the bridge, his breath coming in heavy gasps. "Thank you, Elara," he said, his voice filled with gratitude.

Elara smiled, her eyes reflecting the depth of her feelings. "We're in this together, Aiden. I'll always be here for you."

They continued across the bridge, their trust in each other unwavering. When they finally reached the other side, they took a moment to catch their breath and reflect on the journey so far.

Finding Strength in Unity

AS THEY VENTURED DEEPER into the forest, the landscape grew more treacherous and the challenges more daunting. They faced enchanted beasts, navigated through fields of poisonous plants, and encountered malevolent spirits that sought to hinder their progress.

Each challenge tested their skills and their bond, but they faced them with a renewed sense of unity and determination. They learned to rely on each other's strengths, finding ways to complement and support one another.

One night, as they rested in a hidden glade, Aiden and Elara found themselves reflecting on their journey and the growth they had experienced together.

"Aiden," Elara said softly, her voice filled with warmth, "I never imagined that our journey would take us here. Despite everything we've faced, I feel like we've come out stronger."

Aiden nodded, his eyes reflecting the same sentiment. "I agree, Elara. Our bond has been tested, but it's only made us more resilient. I have faith in us and in the future we're building together."

Elara's heart swelled with love and gratitude. "Thank you, Aiden. Your faith means the world to me. Together, we can overcome anything."

As they sat by the fire, the warmth and light creating a sense of comfort and safety, they felt a renewed sense of hope and determination. Their journey was far from over, but they faced the future with a deep sense of unity and love.

The Final Stretch

WITH EACH PASSING DAY, Aiden and Elara grew closer to their goal. The forest seemed to grow darker and more foreboding, the air heavy with the lingering presence of Malakar's dark magic. They knew that they were nearing the sorcerer's lair, and their resolve only strengthened with each step.

One evening, as they set up camp near a secluded grove, they felt a palpable sense of anticipation. The journey had been long and arduous, but they were now on the brink of confronting the source of the darkness that threatened their world.

As they prepared for the final leg of their journey, Aiden and Elara took a moment to reflect on their experiences and the bond that had grown between them.

"Aiden," Elara said, her voice filled with emotion, "no matter what happens tomorrow, I want you to know how much I love you. Our journey has been filled with challenges, but it has also brought us closer together."

Aiden reached out, taking her hand in his. "I love you too, Elara. We have faced so much, and I know that we can face whatever comes our way. Together, we are unstoppable."

They embraced, their hearts filled with a sense of unity and purpose. As they looked out at the darkened forest, they knew that their journey was far from over, but they faced it with a deep sense of hope and determination.

The Lair of Malakar

THE FOLLOWING MORNING, Aiden and Elara set out with a renewed sense of purpose. The forest grew darker and more oppressive as they neared Malakar's lair, the air thick with the presence of dark magic. They moved cautiously, their senses heightened and their hearts steeled for the final confrontation.

As they approached the entrance to the lair, they felt a surge of dark energy, a palpable reminder of the power that awaited them. Aiden drew his sword, the blade gleaming with a light that seemed to push back the darkness. Elara raised her hands, her magic crackling with energy as she prepared for the battle ahead.

The entrance to the lair was guarded by twisted statues and enchanted barriers, a testament to Malakar's dark power. Aiden and Elara exchanged a look of determination, knowing that they would need to rely on each other to overcome the challenges that lay ahead.

With a series of precise incantations, Elara shattered the barriers, clearing the way for them to enter. They moved swiftly and silently, their hearts pounding with anticipation as they ventured deeper into the lair.

The corridors were filled with shadows and echoes, the air thick with the scent of decay and dark magic. As they navigated the labyrinthine passages, they encountered Malakar's minions—shadowy creatures that lurked in the darkness, ready to attack.

Aiden and Elara fought valiantly, their movements synchronized and their hearts united in their determination to reach Malakar. The battles were fierce and relentless, but they pressed on, driven by their shared resolve.

Finally, they entered a vast chamber, its walls lined with ancient runes and sigils that pulsed with dark energy. At the center of the chamber stood Malakar, his presence commanding and terrifying. His eyes glowed with malevolent intent as he surveyed the intruders, a sinister smile curling across his lips.

"Welcome," Malakar hissed, his voice echoing through the chamber. "You are brave to come here, but your efforts are futile. I will crush you, and both Eldoria and Ravenspire will fall under my rule."

Aiden stepped forward, his sword raised defiantly. "We will never let that happen, Malakar. Your reign of terror ends here."

Elara joined him, her hands crackling with magical energy. "We will fight for our homes, our people, and for the light that still shines in this world."

Malakar laughed, a chilling sound that sent shivers down their spines. "Very well. Let us see if your courage matches your words."

The Final Battle

THE BATTLE THAT ENSUED was one of epic proportions, a clash of light and darkness that shook the very foundations of the lair. Aiden and Elara fought side by side, their movements synchronized and their hearts united in their determination to defeat Malakar.

Aiden's sword glowed with a brilliant light, each strike infused with the power of the enchanted amulet around his neck. He moved with precision and strength, parrying Malakar's dark magic and countering with powerful blows.

Elara's magic was a force to be reckoned with, her spells weaving through the air with a grace and intensity that left their enemies reeling. She summoned elemental forces, conjuring flames and lightning to strike at Malakar and his minions.

The other knights and witches joined the fray, their combined efforts creating a formidable force that pushed Malakar to his limits. The chamber was filled with the sounds of clashing steel and crackling magic, the air thick with the scent of ozone and the acrid tang of dark energy.

Despite their best efforts, Malakar proved to be a formidable opponent. His dark magic was powerful and relentless, and he seemed to draw strength from the very shadows that surrounded him. He unleashed waves of dark energy, forcing Aiden and Elara to fight with every ounce of their strength and skill.

Aiden felt the strain of the battle weighing on him, but he refused to give in. He glanced at Elara, her face set with determination, and drew strength from the bond they shared. Together, they could overcome any obstacle.

With a surge of resolve, Aiden pressed forward, his sword blazing with light as he launched a fierce assault on Malakar. Elara joined him, her magic intertwining with his attacks to create a devastating combination of light and power.

Malakar snarled in frustration, his defenses weakening under the relentless onslaught. Aiden and Elara pressed their advantage, their hearts and minds united in their goal.

Finally, with a powerful strike, Aiden's sword pierced Malakar's defenses, the blade sinking deep into the dark sorcerer's chest. Malakar let out a scream of rage and pain, his body convulsing as the light of the enchanted amulet overwhelmed his dark magic.

Elara raised her hands, casting a final incantation that channeled the combined power of the group into a concentrated blast of light. The chamber was filled with a blinding radiance, and Malakar's form disintegrated, his dark essence consumed by the light.

As the light faded, the chamber grew quiet, the oppressive darkness lifting to reveal the weary but triumphant faces of the group. Aiden and Elara stood together, their hearts filled with relief and gratitude.

Healing and Reconciliation

THE DEFEAT OF MALAKAR marked the end of their perilous journey, but the path to healing and reconciliation was just beginning. Aiden and Elara returned to Eldoria, their hearts filled with a renewed sense of hope and determination.

As they walked through the forest, the trees whispered their blessings, and the magic of Eldoria embraced them. They knew that their bond had been tested and strained, but it had emerged stronger and more resilient.

One evening, as they sat by the campfire, Aiden took Elara's hand and looked into her eyes. "Elara, we've been through so much together. Our love has faced trials and challenges, but it has only grown stronger. I want to spend the rest of my life with you, facing whatever comes our way."

Elara's heart swelled with love and joy. "Aiden, I feel the same. Our journey is just beginning, and I want to walk it with you by my side."

With their hearts united, Aiden and Elara pledged to continue their quest to protect the enchanted forest and its inhabitants. They knew that their love was a powerful force, one that could overcome any obstacle and bring light to the darkest of times.

As they walked hand in hand through the forest, the trees whispered their blessings, and the magic of Eldoria embraced them. They were ready to face whatever challenges lay ahead, secure in the knowledge that their love was true and unwavering.

Together, they would forge a future filled with hope, love, and magic, their hearts bound by a bond that was as powerful and enduring as the enchanted forest itself.

Chapter 9: The Hidden Village

The Witch's Love Spell

AIDEN AND ELARA MOVED through the forest, their steps slow and deliberate. The recent battles had taken their toll on both of them, physically and emotionally. Their hearts were heavy with the realization that, while Malakar had been temporarily thwarted, his dark magic still threatened Eldoria and Ravenspire. They needed a place to rest, regroup, and plan their next move.

Sanctuary: The Hidden Village

THE FOREST GREW DENSER, the trees taller and their branches intertwining to form a canopy that blocked out the sun. They followed a faint path, hoping it would lead them to a place of safety. As they walked, the air around them began to shimmer with a soft, golden light. They sensed a presence, ancient and powerful, watching over them.

Suddenly, the path opened into a clearing, revealing a hidden village nestled among the trees. The village was unlike any they had ever seen, with houses made of living wood and stone, blending seamlessly into the natural surroundings. The air was filled with the scent of blooming flowers and the sound of gentle streams.

Aiden and Elara exchanged a look of wonder and relief. They had stumbled upon a sanctuary, a place where they could find refuge and perhaps the answers they sought.

As they entered the village, they were greeted by a group of friendly magical beings. These beings, known as the Eldari, were tall and graceful, with eyes that shimmered with an inner light. Their presence was calming and reassuring, and Aiden and Elara felt a sense of peace wash over them.

One of the Eldari, a wise and gentle leader named Liora, stepped forward to greet them. Her eyes, filled with kindness and understanding, met theirs.

"Welcome to Elarindor," Liora said, her voice melodic and soothing. "We have been expecting you."

Aiden and Elara exchanged a look of surprise. "Expecting us?" Aiden asked, his voice filled with curiosity.

Liora nodded. "Yes, the spirits of the forest have spoken to us of your journey and the trials you have faced. We are here to help you find the answers you seek and to provide you with the sanctuary you need."

Elara felt a surge of hope. "Thank you, Liora. We are grateful for your hospitality and your guidance."

Knowledge: Learning About the Sorcerer's Weakness and Elara's Powers

OVER THE NEXT FEW DAYS, Aiden and Elara found solace and rest in the hidden village of Elarindor. The Eldari shared their knowledge and wisdom, teaching them about the ancient magic that flowed through the forest and the true nature of their powers.

One evening, as they sat around a fire in the village's central gathering place, Liora began to speak of Malakar and his dark magic.

"Malakar was once one of us," she said, her voice tinged with sadness. "He was a powerful sorcerer, gifted with great magic. But his heart was filled with ambition and a hunger for power. He sought to control the magic of Eldoria, bending it to his will. When he was unable to do so, he turned to dark magic, corrupting the natural balance of the forest."

Aiden listened intently, his brow furrowed in thought. "How can we stop him, Liora? His power is immense, and his dark magic seems to grow stronger every day."

Liora's eyes met his, filled with a deep wisdom. "Malakar's power is great, but it is not without its weaknesses. His dark magic is fueled by fear and hatred. If we can disrupt the source of his power, we can weaken him and make him vulnerable."

Elara leaned forward, her eyes shining with determination. "What is the source of his power, and how can we disrupt it?"

Liora gestured to a nearby elder, an ancient being named Elandor, who stepped forward to share his knowledge. "The source of Malakar's power lies in a dark artifact known as the Shadow Crystal. It is a relic of immense dark magic, capable of corrupting and controlling the natural energies of the forest. If we can destroy the Shadow Crystal, we can strip Malakar of his power."

Aiden and Elara exchanged a look of determination. They had faced many challenges, but this would be their most dangerous mission yet. They needed a plan, and they needed to understand their own powers fully.

Elandor turned to Elara, his eyes filled with curiosity and respect. "Elara, there is something unique about your magic. It is connected to the very essence of the forest. You possess an ancient power that few have ever known. To defeat Malakar, you must fully embrace and understand this power."

Elara felt a sense of awe and responsibility. "How do I do that, Elandor? How can I harness this power to help us defeat Malakar?"

Elandor smiled gently. "You must undertake a journey of self-discovery. There is a sacred grove deep within the forest, a place where the magic of Eldoria is at its strongest. There, you will find the answers you seek and the strength you need."

Plan: Formulating a Plan to Confront the Sorcerer

WITH THE KNOWLEDGE of Malakar's weakness and the true nature of Elara's powers, Aiden and Elara began to formulate a plan to confront the dark sorcerer. They gathered the Eldari, the witches, and the knights, each bringing their unique strengths and abilities to the table.

"We need to approach this strategically," Aiden said, his voice firm and commanding. "Our first priority is to locate the Shadow Crystal and destroy it. Without it, Malakar will be significantly weakened."

Elara nodded in agreement. "While Aiden and I search for the Shadow Crystal, the rest of you will need to create a diversion. Draw Malakar's attention away from us and keep his forces occupied."

Liora stepped forward, her eyes filled with determination. "The Eldari will aid you in this. We know the forest well and can use our magic to create illusions and obstacles to confuse and delay Malakar's minions."

Aiden and Elara exchanged a look of gratitude. "Thank you, Liora. Your help is invaluable," Aiden said.

Elandor raised a hand, drawing their attention. "Elara, before you embark on this journey, you must visit the sacred grove. It is there that you will find the guidance and strength you need to face Malakar."

Elara nodded, her heart filled with resolve. "I will go to the grove and return as soon as I can. Aiden, will you come with me?"

Aiden's eyes softened as he looked at her. "Of course, Elara. We'll face this together."

With their plan in place, Aiden and Elara prepared for their journey to the sacred grove. They gathered supplies and said their farewells to the villagers of Elarindor, grateful for the sanctuary and knowledge they had found.

Journey to the Sacred Grove

THE JOURNEY TO THE sacred grove was arduous and filled with challenges. The forest seemed to grow darker and more foreboding as they ventured deeper, the air heavy with an ancient magic that both guided and tested them.

As they walked, Aiden and Elara spoke of their hopes and fears, their bond growing stronger with each step. The trust and understanding they had built in Elarindor gave them the strength to face the unknown together.

One night, as they camped near a shimmering lake, Elara turned to Aiden, her eyes reflecting the starlit sky. "Aiden, do you ever wonder what our lives would be like if we hadn't been drawn into this battle? If we could just be together, without the weight of the world on our shoulders?"

Aiden smiled, his heart filled with love for her. "I do, Elara. But I believe that our love is stronger because of the challenges we've faced. We've grown and learned so much together. And when this is over, we'll have the chance to build the life we've always dreamed of."

Elara's heart swelled with hope. "I believe that too, Aiden. And I promise that we'll find a way to defeat Malakar and protect our world. Together."

Embracing the Power

AS THEY NEARED THE sacred grove, the air grew lighter, and a sense of tranquility enveloped them. The grove was a place of unparalleled beauty, with ancient trees that seemed to touch the sky and a shimmering pool at its center. The magic of the forest pulsed through the air, filling them with a sense of awe and reverence.

Elara stepped forward, her heart pounding with anticipation. She could feel the power of the grove calling to her, inviting her to embrace her true potential. Aiden stood by her side, his presence a comforting anchor.

"Elara," Aiden said softly, "you are stronger than you know. Trust in yourself and the magic within you. I believe in you."

Elara took a deep breath, her eyes closing as she focused on the magic of the grove. She felt the energy of the forest flowing through her, connecting her to the very essence of Eldoria. As she opened her eyes, they glowed with a radiant light, a testament to the power she now wielded.

With a sense of purpose and determination, Elara stepped into the pool at the center of the grove. The water was cool and soothing, and as she waded deeper, she felt the magic of the forest enveloping her, guiding her towards the answers she sought.

The Vision

AS ELARA STOOD IN THE center of the pool, she closed her eyes and allowed the magic of the grove to flow through her. She felt a sense of connection and unity with the forest, as if she were a part of its very essence.

Suddenly, a vision filled her mind. She saw the Shadow Crystal, a dark and twisted artifact pulsing with malevolent energy. She saw Malakar, his eyes filled with hatred and ambition, drawing power from the crystal and spreading his dark magic throughout the forest.

But then, the vision shifted. She saw herself and Aiden, standing together, their combined light and magic shining brightly. She saw the crystal shatter, its dark energy dissipating into the air. And she saw Malakar, weakened and vulnerable, his dark reign finally brought to an end.

As the vision faded, Elara opened her eyes, her heart filled with a sense of clarity and purpose. She knew what needed to be done, and she was ready to face the challenges ahead.

Returning to the Village

WITH THE KNOWLEDGE of Malakar's weakness and the true nature of her powers, Elara returned to the village with Aiden by her side. They shared their findings with the Eldari, the witches, and the knights, and together they refined their plan to confront the dark sorcerer.

"We know that the Shadow Crystal is the source of Malakar's power," Elara explained, her voice filled with determination. "If we can destroy it, we can weaken him and make him vulnerable. But we must act quickly and strategically."

Aiden nodded, his eyes reflecting the same resolve. "Our plan remains the same. Elara and I will search for the Shadow Crystal and destroy it. The rest of you will create a diversion to keep Malakar's forces occupied."

Liora stepped forward, her eyes filled with confidence. "The Eldari will aid you in this. We will use our magic to create illusions and obstacles, buying you the time you need to reach the crystal."

Elandor raised a hand, drawing their attention. "Elara, your journey to the sacred grove has unlocked a great power within you. Use that power to guide and protect you. Trust in yourself and in the bond you share with Aiden."

Elara felt a sense of gratitude and responsibility. "Thank you, Elandor. I will do everything in my power to ensure our success."

With their plan in place, Aiden and Elara prepared for the final confrontation with Malakar. They knew that the journey ahead would be fraught with danger, but they were ready to face it together.

The Final Confrontation

THE DAY OF THE FINAL confrontation dawned with a sense of anticipation and resolve. Aiden and Elara, accompanied by the Eldari, the witches, and the knights, made their way towards Malakar's lair. The air was thick with tension, the forest holding its breath in anticipation of the battle to come.

As they approached the lair, they could feel the presence of Malakar's dark magic, a palpable force that sought to deter and intimidate them. But their determination and unity gave them strength, and they pressed on with unwavering resolve.

At the entrance to the lair, Liora and the Eldari began their work, creating powerful illusions and obstacles to confuse and delay Malakar's forces. The witches and knights stood ready to defend and protect, their hearts filled with courage and determination.

Aiden and Elara moved swiftly and silently through the lair, their senses heightened and their minds focused on their mission. They encountered numerous obstacles and challenges, each one testing their resolve and their bond. But they faced each challenge with strength and unity, drawing on the power of the forest and their love for each other.

Finally, they reached the heart of the lair, where the Shadow Crystal pulsed with dark energy. Malakar stood before it, his eyes filled with rage and hatred.

"You have come far," Malakar hissed, his voice filled with venom. "But you will go no further. My power is absolute, and you will fall before me."

Aiden raised his sword, the blade glowing with a brilliant light. "We will never let that happen, Malakar. Your reign of terror ends here."

Elara stepped forward, her hands crackling with magical energy. "Your dark magic has no place in this world. We will destroy the Shadow Crystal and strip you of your power."

With a furious roar, Malakar unleashed a wave of dark energy, seeking to overwhelm and destroy them. But Aiden and Elara stood firm, their combined light and magic creating a shield that deflected the attack.

They moved together, their movements synchronized and their hearts united in their determination to defeat Malakar. Aiden's sword struck with precision and power, each blow weakening the sorcerer's defenses. Elara's magic wove through the air with a grace and intensity that left Malakar reeling.

The battle was fierce and relentless, but Aiden and Elara pressed on, their resolve unbroken. Finally, with a powerful strike, Aiden's sword pierced the

Shadow Crystal, shattering it into a thousand pieces. The dark energy dissipated into the air, and Malakar let out a scream of rage and pain.

Elara raised her hands, casting a final incantation that channeled the combined power of the forest and their bond into a concentrated blast of light. The chamber was filled with a blinding radiance, and Malakar's form disintegrated, his dark essence consumed by the light.

Victory and Reflection

AS THE LIGHT FADED, the chamber grew quiet, the oppressive darkness lifting to reveal the weary but triumphant faces of Aiden and Elara. They had done it. They had defeated Malakar and destroyed the source of his dark power.

They made their way back to the entrance of the lair, where they were greeted by the Eldari, the witches, and the knights. The air was filled with a sense of relief and celebration, their hearts filled with gratitude and hope.

Liora stepped forward, her eyes filled with pride. "You have done it. The darkness has been vanquished, and the forest is safe once more. We are forever grateful for your bravery and your sacrifice."

Aiden and Elara exchanged a look of gratitude and love. "We could not have done it without all of you," Aiden said, his voice filled with sincerity. "Thank you for standing with us and for believing in us."

Elara nodded, her heart swelling with emotion. "Together, we have shown that love and light can overcome even the darkest of forces. We are stronger because of the bond we share and the unity we have found."

A New Beginning

WITH MALAKAR DEFEATED and the Shadow Crystal destroyed, Aiden and Elara returned to the hidden village of Elarindor. They were greeted with joy and celebration, their hearts filled with a sense of peace and fulfillment.

As they walked hand in hand through the village, they felt a deep sense of connection and purpose. They had faced great challenges and overcome immense obstacles, but their love had guided them through it all.

One evening, as they stood by the shimmering pool in the sacred grove, Aiden turned to Elara, his eyes filled with love and devotion. "Elara, our journey has been long and filled with trials, but it has only made our bond stronger. I want to spend the rest of my life with you, building a future filled with hope and love."

Elara's eyes sparkled with joy, and she reached out to take his hand. "Aiden, I feel the same. Our love has endured and grown, and I am ready to face whatever the future holds, as long as we are together."

With their hearts united, Aiden and Elara pledged to continue their quest to protect the enchanted forest and its inhabitants. They knew that their love was a powerful force, one that could overcome any obstacle and bring light to the darkest of times.

As they walked hand in hand through the forest, the trees whispered their blessings, and the magic of Eldoria embraced them. They were ready to face whatever challenges lay ahead, secure in the knowledge that their love was true and unwavering.

Together, they would forge a future filled with hope, love, and magic, their hearts bound by a bond that was as powerful and enduring as the enchanted forest itself.

Chapter 10: The Battle Preparations

The Witch's Love Spell

The tranquil village of Elarindor was alive with activity as Aiden and Elara prepared for the upcoming battle. The defeat of Malakar had not eradicated the threat entirely, for his followers and dark magic still lingered in the shadows of Eldoria. The sorcerer's influence continued to spread, and Aiden and Elara knew that a final confrontation was inevitable. They had to be ready, and that meant training, gathering allies, and fortifying their defenses.

Training: Preparing for Battle

AIDEN AND ELARA SPENT their days training rigorously, honing their skills and preparing for the challenges ahead. The Eldari, with their vast knowledge of magic and combat, guided them through advanced techniques and strategies. Each day brought new lessons and new strengths, and they pushed themselves to the limits, determined to be ready for whatever lay ahead.

In the heart of the village, a large clearing served as their training ground. Aiden practiced his swordsmanship with the Eldari warriors, his movements becoming more fluid and precise with each passing day. The Eldari's unique combat techniques, which combined agility and magical energy, enhanced his abilities and made him a formidable opponent.

Elara, meanwhile, focused on mastering her magical powers. She worked closely with Liora and Elandor, learning to harness the ancient magic of the forest and channel it into powerful spells. Her connection to the forest deepened, and she discovered new abilities that she had never imagined. She could now summon elemental forces, heal wounds with a touch, and create protective barriers of light.

Their training sessions were intense but rewarding. Aiden and Elara found themselves growing stronger and more confident, their bond deepening with each shared challenge. They learned to rely on each other's strengths and to support each other in moments of weakness.

Emotional Growth: Confronting Their Feelings and Regret

DESPITE THEIR PROGRESS, there was an emotional weight that lingered between them. The memory of the love spell and the betrayal it represented had not been fully resolved. Elara's regret weighed heavily on her heart, and she knew that they needed to confront these feelings if they were to move forward united and strong.

One evening, after a particularly grueling training session, Aiden and Elara sat by the fire, the warmth and light creating a comforting cocoon around them. The village was quiet, the Eldari having retreated to their homes for the night. The air was filled with the scent of pine and the gentle rustling of leaves.

Elara took a deep breath, her heart pounding with a mix of fear and determination. She knew that it was time to address the unresolved issues between them. She turned to Aiden, her eyes filled with sincerity and vulnerability.

"Aiden, there's something I need to talk to you about," she began, her voice trembling slightly. "It's about the love spell. I know we've touched on it before, but I feel like we haven't fully addressed it. I need you to understand how deeply sorry I am for what I did."

Aiden looked at her, his expression thoughtful and compassionate. "Elara, I know you regret casting the spell. And I understand why you did it. But I also know that our love is real, and it has grown stronger because of everything we've been through."

Elara's eyes filled with tears, and she reached out to take his hand. "I was so afraid of losing you, Aiden. I let my fear cloud my judgment, and I made a terrible mistake. I never wanted to manipulate you or take away your free will. I just wanted to protect what we had."

Aiden squeezed her hand gently, his eyes reflecting the depth of his feelings. "I know, Elara. And I forgive you. We've faced so many challenges together, and we've come out stronger on the other side. I believe in us, and I believe in our love."

Elara felt a sense of relief and gratitude wash over her. "Thank you, Aiden. Your forgiveness means everything to me. I promise to always be honest and open with you, to trust in the love we share."

Aiden smiled, his heart swelling with love and pride. "And I promise to always stand by your side, to support you and love you, no matter what challenges we face."

Gathering Allies

WITH THEIR EMOTIONAL bond strengthened and their skills honed, Aiden and Elara turned their attention to gathering allies for the upcoming battle. They knew that they could not defeat Malakar and his followers alone; they needed the support of the Eldari, the witches, and the knights of Ravenspire.

Liora and Elandor worked tirelessly to rally the Eldari, their wisdom and leadership inspiring confidence and determination. The Eldari, with their deep connection to the forest and their formidable magical abilities, were invaluable allies in the fight against darkness.

Aiden reached out to the knights of Ravenspire, sending messages to his comrades and calling for their support. The knights, loyal and brave, responded with unwavering resolve. They understood the gravity of the situation and were ready to stand by Aiden's side in the battle to come.

Elara communicated with the witches of Eldoria, her messages carried on the winds and through the whispers of the trees. The witches, guardians of ancient magic and protectors of the forest, answered her call. They brought with them their knowledge of spells and potions, their hearts united in the fight against Malakar's dark magic.

As their allies gathered in Elarindor, the village became a hub of activity and preparation. The Eldari worked alongside the knights and witches, sharing their knowledge and skills. Training sessions were held, strategies were discussed, and plans were formulated. The sense of unity and purpose was palpable, and Aiden and Elara felt a renewed sense of hope and determination.

Confronting Their Feelings

AMIDST THE FLURRY OF preparations, Aiden and Elara found moments of quiet reflection, where they could confront their feelings and strengthen their emotional bond. One evening, as they sat by the shimmering pool in the sacred grove, they spoke openly and honestly about their fears, hopes, and dreams.

"Aiden," Elara began, her voice soft and contemplative, "I've been thinking a lot about everything we've been through. The challenges we've faced, the mistakes we've made, and the love we've found. It's been a long and difficult journey, but I believe it has made us stronger."

Aiden nodded, his eyes filled with love and understanding. "I agree, Elara. Our journey has tested us in ways we never imagined, but it has also shown us the depth of our love and our resilience. We've grown so much together, and I believe that we can overcome anything as long as we're united."

Elara smiled, her heart swelling with gratitude. "Thank you, Aiden. Your faith in us means everything to me. I know that we have a difficult battle ahead, but I believe that our love and our bond will guide us through."

Aiden reached out, taking her hand in his. "I believe that too, Elara. We've faced darkness before, and we've always come out stronger. Together, we can defeat Malakar and protect our world."

Their conversation was filled with warmth and sincerity, their hearts open and vulnerable. They spoke of their fears and doubts, their hopes and dreams, and the strength they found in each other. With each word, they felt their bond deepen, their love growing stronger and more resilient.

Formulating the Plan

WITH THEIR EMOTIONAL bond strengthened and their allies gathered, Aiden and Elara turned their attention to formulating the plan for the upcoming battle. They knew that the key to victory lay in their ability to work together, to combine their strengths and overcome Malakar's dark magic.

The leaders of the Eldari, the witches, and the knights gathered in the village's central hall, their faces serious and determined. Maps and charts were spread out on the table, and the air was filled with the hum of magical energy and the clinking of armor.

Aiden stood at the head of the table, his voice steady and commanding. "We know that Malakar's power is fueled by the Shadow Crystal. Our primary objective is to locate and destroy the crystal, which will weaken him and make him vulnerable."

Elara nodded, her eyes reflecting the same determination. "While Aiden and I focus on the crystal, the rest of you will need to create a diversion. Draw Malakar's attention away from us and keep his forces occupied."

Liora stepped forward, her voice filled with confidence. "The Eldari will use our magic to create illusions and obstacles, confusing and delaying Malakar's minions. We will also provide support to the knights and witches in the field."

Elandor raised a hand, drawing their attention. "The witches will use our knowledge of spells and potions to protect and heal our allies. We will also work to disrupt Malakar's dark magic, weakening his hold on the forest."

Aiden and Elara exchanged a look of gratitude. "Thank you, all of you," Aiden said. "Your support and bravery are invaluable. Together, we will defeat Malakar and protect our world."

With their plan in place, the leaders dispersed to their respective groups, sharing the details and rallying their allies. The village buzzed with activity as preparations were made, weapons were sharpened, and spells were practiced.

Final Preparations

AS THE DAY OF THE BATTLE approached, Aiden and Elara took time to reflect on their journey and their bond. They knew that the upcoming battle would be their greatest challenge yet, but they faced it with a sense of unity and determination.

One evening, as they stood on a hill overlooking the village, Aiden turned to Elara, his eyes filled with love and resolve. "Elara, no matter what happens tomorrow, I want you to know how much I love you. Our journey has been long and difficult, but it has also been filled with moments of joy and growth. I am proud to stand by your side."

Elara's eyes filled with tears, and she reached out to take his hand. "I love you too, Aiden. You have been my strength and my guide, and I am grateful for every moment we've shared. Together, we will face whatever comes our way."

As they embraced, the stars shone brightly above them, a reminder of the light and hope that guided them. They knew that their love was a powerful force, one that could overcome any obstacle and bring light to the darkest of times.

The Night Before the Battle

THE NIGHT BEFORE THE battle was filled with a sense of anticipation and reflection. The village was quiet, the air filled with a sense of calm before the storm. Aiden and Elara took time to connect with their allies, sharing stories and words of encouragement.

They visited the knights, who were sharpening their swords and preparing their armor. Aiden spoke to them with words of courage and resolve, his presence a beacon of strength and determination.

They visited the witches, who were brewing potions and practicing spells. Elara shared her knowledge and wisdom, her voice filled with confidence and hope.

Finally, they visited the Eldari, who were meditating and connecting with the magic of the forest. Liora and Elandor spoke to them with words of guidance and support, their eyes filled with wisdom and love.

As the night deepened, Aiden and Elara returned to the sacred grove, their hearts filled with a sense of peace and unity. They sat by the shimmering pool, their hands intertwined, their love a source of strength and comfort.

"Aiden," Elara said softly, "I believe in us. I believe that our love and our bond will guide us through the challenges ahead. Together, we will defeat Malakar and protect our world."

Aiden smiled, his heart swelling with love and pride. "I believe in us too, Elara. We have faced darkness before, and we have always come out stronger. Together, we are unstoppable."

As they looked out at the stars, they felt a deep sense of connection and purpose. They knew that the battle ahead would be difficult, but they faced it with a sense of hope and determination. Their love was a powerful force, one that could overcome any obstacle and bring light to the darkest of times.

The Morning of the Battle

THE MORNING OF THE battle dawned with a sense of anticipation and resolve. The village was alive with activity as final preparations were made. The air was filled with the hum of magical energy and the clinking of armor, the scent of pine and the sound of rustling leaves.

Aiden and Elara stood at the head of their allies, their hearts filled with a sense of unity and determination. They exchanged a look of love and resolve, their bond a source of strength and comfort.

"Today, we fight for our world," Aiden said, his voice steady and commanding. "We fight for the light and for the love that guides us. Together, we will defeat Malakar and protect Eldoria and Ravenspire."

Elara nodded, her eyes filled with confidence and hope. "Our love is our strength, and our unity is our power. Together, we will overcome the darkness and bring light to our world."

As their allies cheered and rallied around them, Aiden and Elara felt a deep sense of connection and purpose. They knew that the battle ahead would be their greatest challenge yet, but they faced it with a sense of hope and determination.

Together, they would forge a future filled with hope, love, and magic, their hearts bound by a bond that was as powerful and enduring as the enchanted forest itself.

The Battle Begins

AS THE SUN ROSE OVER Eldoria, casting a golden light over the forest, Aiden and Elara led their allies into battle. The air was filled with the sound of swords clashing, spells crackling, and the cries of courage and determination.

The Eldari used their magic to create illusions and obstacles, confusing and delaying Malakar's minions. The knights fought bravely, their swords gleaming in the light as they defended and protected their allies. The witches cast powerful spells, their magic a force of light and hope.

Aiden and Elara moved through the battlefield with precision and strength, their movements synchronized and their hearts united in their determination to defeat Malakar. They faced numerous challenges and obstacles, each one testing their resolve and their bond.

Finally, they reached the heart of Malakar's lair, where the Shadow Crystal pulsed with dark energy. Malakar stood before it, his eyes filled with rage and hatred.

"You have come far," Malakar hissed, his voice filled with venom. "But you will go no further. My power is absolute, and you will fall before me."

Aiden raised his sword, the blade glowing with a brilliant light. "We will never let that happen, Malakar. Your reign of terror ends here."

Elara stepped forward, her hands crackling with magical energy. "Your dark magic has no place in this world. We will destroy the Shadow Crystal and strip you of your power."

With a furious roar, Malakar unleashed a wave of dark energy, seeking to overwhelm and destroy them. But Aiden and Elara stood firm, their combined light and magic creating a shield that deflected the attack.

They moved together, their movements synchronized and their hearts united in their determination to defeat Malakar. Aiden's sword struck with precision and power, each blow weakening the sorcerer's defenses. Elara's magic wove through the air with a grace and intensity that left Malakar reeling.

The battle was fierce and relentless, but Aiden and Elara pressed on, their resolve unbroken. Finally, with a powerful strike, Aiden's sword pierced the Shadow Crystal, shattering it into a thousand pieces. The dark energy dissipated into the air, and Malakar let out a scream of rage and pain.

Elara raised her hands, casting a final incantation that channeled the combined power of the forest and their bond into a concentrated blast of light. The chamber was filled with a blinding radiance, and Malakar's form disintegrated, his dark essence consumed by the light.

Victory and Reflection

AS THE LIGHT FADED, the chamber grew quiet, the oppressive darkness lifting to reveal the weary but triumphant faces of Aiden and Elara. They had done it. They had defeated Malakar and destroyed the source of his dark power.

They made their way back to the entrance of the lair, where they were greeted by the Eldari, the witches, and the knights. The air was filled with a sense of relief and celebration, their hearts filled with gratitude and hope.

Liora stepped forward, her eyes filled with pride. "You have done it. The darkness has been vanquished, and the forest is safe once more. We are forever grateful for your bravery and your sacrifice."

Aiden and Elara exchanged a look of gratitude and love. "We could not have done it without all of you," Aiden said, his voice filled with sincerity. "Thank you for standing with us and for believing in us."

Elara nodded, her heart swelling with emotion. "Together, we have shown that love and light can overcome even the darkest of forces. We are stronger because of the bond we share and the unity we have found."

A New Beginning

WITH MALAKAR DEFEATED and the Shadow Crystal destroyed, Aiden and Elara returned to the hidden village of Elarindor. They were greeted with joy and celebration, their hearts filled with a sense of peace and fulfillment.

As they walked hand in hand through the village, they felt a deep sense of connection and purpose. They had faced great challenges and overcome immense obstacles, but their love had guided them through it all.

One evening, as they stood by the shimmering pool in the sacred grove, Aiden turned to Elara, his eyes filled with love and devotion. "Elara, our journey has been long and filled with trials, but it has only made our bond stronger. I want to spend the rest of my life with you, building a future filled with hope and love."

Elara's eyes sparkled with joy, and she reached out to take his hand. "Aiden, I feel the same. Our love has endured and grown, and I am ready to face whatever the future holds, as long as we are together."

With their hearts united, Aiden and Elara pledged to continue their quest to protect the enchanted forest and its inhabitants. They knew that their love was a powerful force, one that could overcome any obstacle and bring light to the darkest of times.

As they walked hand in hand through the forest, the trees whispered their blessings, and the magic of Eldoria embraced them. They were ready to face whatever challenges lay ahead, secure in the knowledge that their love was true and unwavering.

Together, they would forge a future filled with hope, love, and magic, their hearts bound by a bond that was as powerful and enduring as the enchanted forest itself.

Chapter 11: The Confrontation

The Witch's Love Spell

The sun rose over the enchanted forest of Eldoria, casting a golden light that filtered through the dense canopy of trees. The air was thick with anticipation and a sense of urgency as Aiden, Elara, and their gathered allies prepared for the final confrontation with the dark sorcerer Malakar. They knew that the battle ahead would be their greatest challenge yet, but they faced it with unwavering resolve and a united front.

Showdown: The Epic Battle Against the Dark Sorcerer

THE VILLAGE OF ELARINDOR was a hive of activity as the Eldari, witches, and knights made their final preparations. Weapons were sharpened, spells were practiced, and strategies were reviewed. Aiden and Elara stood at the heart of the village, their eyes reflecting the gravity of the situation and the determination that burned within them.

As the sun reached its zenith, casting a warm glow over the forest, Aiden and Elara led their allies towards Malakar's lair. The path before them was treacherous, filled with dark magic and the remnants of Malakar's minions. The air grew colder and more oppressive as they neared the heart of the dark sorcerer's domain, a palpable reminder of the power they were about to face.

The entrance to Malakar's lair loomed before them, a cavernous opening guarded by grotesque statues and enchanted barriers. The ground trembled beneath their feet, and the air crackled with dark energy. Aiden and Elara exchanged a determined glance, their hearts united in their mission.

"We will not falter," Aiden said, his voice steady and resolute. "Together, we will defeat Malakar and bring light to this world."

Elara nodded, her eyes filled with unwavering resolve. "Our love and our bond are our greatest strengths. We will fight for each other and for the future we believe in."

With a series of precise incantations, Elara shattered the enchanted barriers, clearing the way for their entry. They moved swiftly and silently, their senses heightened and their minds focused on the task at hand. The corridors of the lair were filled with shadows and echoes, the air thick with the scent of decay and dark magic.

As they ventured deeper into the lair, they encountered Malakar's minions—shadowy creatures twisted by dark magic and driven by a relentless hunger for destruction. Aiden and Elara fought valiantly, their movements synchronized and their hearts united in their determination. Aiden's sword gleamed with a brilliant light, each strike a testament to his skill and strength. Elara's magic crackled with energy, weaving through the air with a grace and intensity that left their enemies reeling.

Despite their best efforts, the battle was fierce and relentless. Malakar's minions were numerous and powerful, their attacks fueled by the dark magic that permeated the lair. Aiden and Elara pushed forward, their resolve unbroken, but they knew that the final confrontation with Malakar would be their greatest test.

Teamwork: Fighting Side by Side

AS THEY REACHED THE heart of the lair, Aiden and Elara found themselves standing before a massive chamber, its walls lined with ancient runes and sigils that pulsed with dark energy. At the center of the chamber stood Malakar, his presence commanding and terrifying. His eyes glowed with malevolent intent as he surveyed the intruders, a sinister smile curling across his lips.

"You have come far," Malakar hissed, his voice echoing through the chamber. "But your journey ends here. My power is absolute, and you will fall before me."

Aiden stepped forward, his sword raised defiantly. "We will never let that happen, Malakar. Your reign of terror ends today."

Elara joined him, her hands crackling with magical energy. "Your dark magic has no place in this world. We will fight for the light and for the love that guides us."

With a furious roar, Malakar unleashed a wave of dark energy, seeking to overwhelm and destroy them. But Aiden and Elara stood firm, their combined light and magic creating a shield that deflected the attack. They moved together, their movements synchronized and their hearts united in their determination to defeat Malakar.

Aiden's sword struck with precision and power, each blow weakening the sorcerer's defenses. Elara's magic wove through the air with a grace and intensity that left Malakar reeling. They fought side by side, their bond and their love giving them the strength to face the darkness.

The chamber was filled with the sounds of clashing steel and crackling magic, the air thick with the scent of ozone and the acrid tang of dark energy. The battle was fierce and unrelenting, but Aiden and Elara pressed on, their resolve unbroken.

Sacrifice: Weakening the Sorcerer

DESPITE THEIR COMBINED strength, Malakar's dark magic was powerful and relentless. He drew strength from the shadows, his attacks growing more ferocious with each passing moment. Aiden and Elara knew that they needed to find a way to weaken him, to strip him of his power and make him vulnerable.

As they fought, Elara sensed a shift in the magical energy of the chamber. She realized that the runes and sigils lining the walls were the source of Malakar's power, drawing energy from the dark magic that permeated the lair. She knew that they needed to disrupt the flow of energy, to break the connection that fueled Malakar's strength.

"Aiden," Elara called out, her voice filled with urgency, "the runes and sigils are the source of his power. We need to disrupt the flow of energy."

Aiden nodded, his eyes reflecting the same determination. "I'll create a distraction. You focus on breaking the connection."

With a surge of resolve, Aiden launched a fierce assault on Malakar, his sword blazing with light as he struck with precision and power. Malakar snarled in frustration, his attention diverted by Aiden's relentless attacks.

Elara seized the opportunity, her hands glowing with magical energy as she focused on the runes and sigils. She chanted a powerful incantation, her voice resonating with the ancient magic of the forest. The air crackled with energy as the runes and sigils began to flicker and fade, their connection to the dark magic weakening.

But Malakar sensed what was happening, and with a furious roar, he unleashed a wave of dark energy aimed directly at Elara. Aiden saw the attack coming and knew that he had to act quickly. Without hesitation, he threw himself in front of Elara, his sword raised to deflect the dark energy.

The impact was devastating. The dark energy collided with Aiden's sword, sending a shockwave through the chamber. Aiden was thrown back, his body hitting the ground with a sickening thud. Elara's heart clenched with fear and anguish as she rushed to his side.

"Aiden!" she cried, her voice filled with desperation. "Are you alright?"

Aiden's eyes fluttered open, his breath ragged and pained. "I'm alright, Elara," he said, his voice weak but determined. "Finish the spell. We need to weaken him."

Tears filled Elara's eyes as she nodded, her heart filled with a mix of sorrow and resolve. She turned back to the runes and sigils, her hands glowing with magical energy as she continued the incantation. The air around her shimmered with light as the runes and sigils flickered and faded, their connection to the dark magic breaking.

With a final surge of energy, Elara completed the incantation, and the runes and sigils shattered, their dark energy dissipating into the air. Malakar let out a scream of rage and pain, his strength waning as the source of his power was destroyed.

The Final Strike

WITH MALAKAR WEAKENED and vulnerable, Aiden and Elara knew that this was their moment to strike. They rose to their feet, their hearts filled with determination and resolve. They moved together, their bond and their love giving them the strength to face the darkness.

Aiden raised his sword, the blade glowing with a brilliant light. "This ends now, Malakar," he said, his voice steady and commanding. "Your reign of terror is over."

Elara's hands crackled with magical energy as she stepped forward. "We fight for the light and for the love that guides us. Together, we will bring an end to your darkness."

With a surge of resolve, Aiden and Elara launched a final assault on Malakar. Aiden's sword struck with precision and power, each blow weakening the sorcerer's defenses. Elara's magic wove through the air with a grace and intensity that left Malakar reeling.

The chamber was filled with a blinding radiance as their combined light and magic overwhelmed Malakar's dark energy. The sorcerer let out a final scream of rage and pain as his form disintegrated, his dark essence consumed by the light.

As the light faded, the chamber grew quiet, the oppressive darkness lifting to reveal the weary but triumphant faces of Aiden and Elara. They had done it. They had defeated Malakar and destroyed the source of his dark power.

Aftermath and Reflection

THE DEFEAT OF MALAKAR marked the end of their greatest challenge, but the path to healing and reconciliation was just beginning. Aiden and Elara made their way back to the entrance of the lair, where they were greeted by the Eldari, the witches, and the knights. The air was filled with a sense of relief and celebration, their hearts filled with gratitude and hope.

Liora stepped forward, her eyes filled with pride. "You have done it. The darkness has been vanquished, and the forest is safe once more. We are forever grateful for your bravery and your sacrifice."

Aiden and Elara exchanged a look of gratitude and love. "We could not have done it without all of you," Aiden said, his voice filled with sincerity. "Thank you for standing with us and for believing in us."

Elara nodded, her heart swelling with emotion. "Together, we have shown that love and light can overcome even the darkest of forces. We are stronger because of the bond we share and the unity we have found."

A New Beginning

WITH MALAKAR DEFEATED and the Shadow Crystal destroyed, Aiden and Elara returned to the hidden village of Elarindor. They were greeted with joy and celebration, their hearts filled with a sense of peace and fulfillment.

As they walked hand in hand through the village, they felt a deep sense of connection and purpose. They had faced great challenges and overcome immense obstacles, but their love had guided them through it all.

One evening, as they stood by the shimmering pool in the sacred grove, Aiden turned to Elara, his eyes filled with love and devotion. "Elara, our journey has been long and filled with trials, but it has only made our bond stronger. I want to spend the rest of my life with you, building a future filled with hope and love."

Elara's eyes sparkled with joy, and she reached out to take his hand. "Aiden, I feel the same. Our love has endured and grown, and I am ready to face whatever the future holds, as long as we are together."

With their hearts united, Aiden and Elara pledged to continue their quest to protect the enchanted forest and its inhabitants. They knew that their love was a powerful force, one that could overcome any obstacle and bring light to the darkest of times.

As they walked hand in hand through the forest, the trees whispered their blessings, and the magic of Eldoria embraced them. They were ready to face whatever challenges lay ahead, secure in the knowledge that their love was true and unwavering.

Together, they would forge a future filled with hope, love, and magic, their hearts bound by a bond that was as powerful and enduring as the enchanted forest itself.

Victory and Celebration

THE VICTORY OVER MALAKAR was celebrated with joy and gratitude in Elarindor. The village was filled with laughter, music, and the warm glow of magical lights. The Eldari, witches, and knights came together to honor the bravery and sacrifice of those who had fought to protect their world.

Aiden and Elara stood at the heart of the celebration, their hearts filled with a sense of fulfillment and hope. They exchanged words of gratitude and love with their allies, their bond and unity a testament to the strength they had found in each other.

As the night deepened, Aiden and Elara found themselves standing by the shimmering pool in the sacred grove, their hearts filled with a sense of peace and contentment. They looked out at the stars, their hands intertwined, their love a source of strength and comfort.

"Aiden," Elara said softly, her voice filled with emotion, "our journey has been long and filled with challenges, but it has also been filled with moments of joy and growth. I am grateful for every moment we've shared, and I am ready to face the future with you by my side."

Aiden smiled, his heart swelling with love and pride. "I feel the same, Elara. Our love has guided us through the darkest of times, and it will continue to guide us as we build a future filled with hope and love."

As they embraced, the stars shone brightly above them, a reminder of the light and hope that guided them. They knew that their love was a powerful force, one that could overcome any obstacle and bring light to the darkest of times.

Together, they would forge a future filled with hope, love, and magic, their hearts bound by a bond that was as powerful and enduring as the enchanted forest itself.

The Road Ahead

WITH MALAKAR DEFEATED and the forest safe once more, Aiden and Elara looked to the future with hope and determination. They knew that their journey was far from over, but they faced it with a sense of unity and purpose.

They continued to work alongside the Eldari, witches, and knights, using their skills and knowledge to protect and heal the land. Their bond and their love remained a source of strength and inspiration, guiding them through the challenges that lay ahead.

As they walked hand in hand through the forest, they felt a deep sense of connection and purpose. They knew that their love was a powerful force, one that could overcome any obstacle and bring light to the darkest of times.

Together, they would forge a future filled with hope, love, and magic, their hearts bound by a bond that was as powerful and enduring as the enchanted forest itself.

Chapter 12: The Aftermath

The Witch's Love Spell

THE ECHOES OF THE FINAL battle against Malakar had faded, leaving behind a quiet, somber stillness in the enchanted forest of Eldoria. The sorcerer was defeated, but the cost had been great. The forest and the kingdom of Ravenspire bore the scars of the conflict, and Aiden and Elara, though victorious, faced the daunting task of healing the wounds left by the darkness that had threatened their world.

Victory: The Sorcerer is Defeated, but at a Great Cost

AS THE SUN ROSE OVER Eldoria, casting a golden light that filtered through the dense canopy of trees, the extent of the devastation became apparent. The once vibrant forest was now a landscape of broken branches and scorched earth, the air heavy with the lingering scent of smoke and dark magic. The village of Elarindor, though spared the worst of the destruction, still showed signs of the battle that had raged around it.

Aiden and Elara stood at the edge of the village, their hearts heavy with the weight of their victory. They had faced the darkness and emerged triumphant, but the cost had been immense. Many lives had been lost, and the land they loved had been scarred by the conflict.

"We did it," Aiden said softly, his voice filled with a mix of relief and sorrow. "Malakar is defeated, but the price was high."

Elara nodded, her eyes reflecting the same mixture of emotions. "We knew it wouldn't be easy. But now, we have the chance to heal and rebuild. We owe it to those who fought and sacrificed to make this victory possible."

The village was a hive of activity as the Eldari, witches, and knights worked to tend to the wounded and repair the damage. The sense of camaraderie and unity that had carried them through the battle now guided their efforts to heal and restore.

Liora, the wise leader of the Eldari, approached Aiden and Elara, her eyes filled with a gentle, understanding light. "You have both shown great courage and strength. The battle may be over, but the work of healing and rebuilding has just begun."

Aiden and Elara exchanged a determined glance. "We are ready to do whatever it takes," Aiden said, his voice steady and resolute. "We will help heal the land and our people."

Healing: The Kingdom and the Enchanted Forest Begin to Heal

THE PROCESS OF HEALING and rebuilding was slow and painstaking, but it was driven by a deep sense of purpose and hope. Aiden and Elara dedicated themselves to the task, working alongside their allies to restore the forest and the kingdom to their former glory.

In the heart of the village, a large clearing served as the center of their efforts. The Eldari, with their deep connection to the forest, used their magic to encourage new growth and cleanse the land of the lingering dark energy. The witches brewed potions and cast healing spells, tending to the wounded and ensuring that the land could once again flourish.

Aiden and Elara worked tirelessly, their roles shifting as needed to address the various challenges they faced. Aiden, with his strength and leadership, organized the knights and villagers, ensuring that everyone had a role to play in the rebuilding efforts. He led teams to clear debris, repair structures, and plant new trees, his presence a source of inspiration and motivation.

Elara, with her deep understanding of magic and the forest, focused on healing the land and its inhabitants. She worked closely with the Eldari and the witches, using her powers to cleanse the dark magic and encourage new growth.

She also tended to the emotional wounds of those who had fought and lost loved ones, offering comfort and support.

One afternoon, as Elara worked to heal a particularly damaged area of the forest, she felt a surge of hope and determination. The land responded to her magic, new shoots and blossoms emerging from the scorched earth. She sensed the forest's gratitude and its willingness to heal and grow, and it filled her with a renewed sense of purpose.

"Aiden," Elara called out, her voice filled with a mix of excitement and relief. "The forest is responding. It wants to heal."

Aiden joined her, his eyes reflecting the same sense of hope. "That's wonderful, Elara. Together, we can restore the forest to its former beauty."

As they continued their work, they found moments of quiet reflection and connection. They spoke of their hopes and dreams, their fears and doubts, and the strength they found in each other. With each passing day, their bond grew stronger, their love a source of comfort and inspiration.

New Beginning: Aiden and Elara's Relationship is Tested and Strengthened

DESPITE THE PROGRESS they made in healing the land and their people, Aiden and Elara faced their own internal struggles. The battle against Malakar had taken a toll on their relationship, and they needed to confront the emotional scars left by the conflict.

One evening, as they sat by the fire in the sacred grove, Aiden turned to Elara, his eyes filled with a mixture of love and uncertainty. "Elara, there's something I've been wanting to talk to you about. The battle against Malakar, the sacrifices we made... it's been weighing heavily on my mind."

Elara looked at him, her heart aching with empathy. "I know, Aiden. It's been difficult for both of us. But we faced it together, and we came out stronger because of it."

Aiden nodded, his expression thoughtful. "I agree. But I also feel like there are things we haven't fully addressed. The love spell, the fear of losing each other... those issues are still there, lingering in the background."

Elara sighed, her eyes reflecting the same concerns. "You're right, Aiden. The love spell was a mistake, and I regret it deeply. But I also believe that it taught us important lessons about trust and vulnerability."

Aiden reached out, taking her hand in his. "I want us to be completely honest with each other, Elara. To confront our fears and doubts head-on, and to strengthen our bond through open communication."

Elara squeezed his hand gently, her heart swelling with love and gratitude. "I want that too, Aiden. Our love is the foundation of everything we do, and I believe that we can overcome any obstacle as long as we face it together."

Over the next few weeks, Aiden and Elara dedicated time to strengthening their relationship. They spoke openly and honestly about their fears and insecurities, their hopes and dreams, and the lessons they had learned from their journey. They practiced forgiveness and empathy, finding new ways to support and uplift each other.

One afternoon, as they walked through the restored forest, Elara turned to Aiden, her eyes filled with a sense of peace and contentment. "Aiden, I feel like we've grown so much together. We've faced incredible challenges, but our love has only deepened and strengthened."

Aiden smiled, his heart swelling with pride and love. "I feel the same, Elara. Our bond is unbreakable, and I know that we can face whatever the future holds, as long as we're together."

As they continued their walk, the forest seemed to come alive around them, the trees and flowers a testament to the healing and growth they had achieved. The air was filled with the scent of blooming flowers and the gentle rustle of leaves, a reminder of the beauty and resilience of the natural world.

Rebuilding the Kingdom

WITH THE FOREST WELL on its way to recovery, Aiden and Elara turned their attention to the kingdom of Ravenspire. The battle against Malakar had left its mark on the kingdom, and they knew that the process of rebuilding would be long and arduous.

The people of Ravenspire, inspired by the bravery and sacrifice of their leaders, rallied together to restore their homes and communities. Aiden and

Elara worked closely with King Alden, coordinating efforts and providing support wherever it was needed.

Aiden's leadership and strategic mind were invaluable in organizing the rebuilding efforts. He led teams to repair infrastructure, rebuild homes, and restore vital services. His presence was a source of strength and motivation for the people, and his dedication to the task inspired confidence and hope.

Elara, with her deep understanding of magic and healing, focused on addressing the emotional and psychological wounds left by the conflict. She worked with the kingdom's healers and counselors, providing support and guidance to those who had lost loved ones or experienced trauma. Her compassion and empathy were a balm for the wounded hearts of the people, and her presence brought a sense of peace and comfort.

One day, as they walked through the bustling streets of Ravenspire, Aiden and Elara marveled at the progress that had been made. The kingdom was beginning to heal, and the sense of unity and purpose that had carried them through the battle now guided their efforts to rebuild.

"Aiden," Elara said, her voice filled with admiration, "you've done an incredible job leading the rebuilding efforts. The people look to you for guidance and strength, and you've risen to the occasion beautifully."

Aiden smiled, his heart swelling with pride and gratitude. "Thank you, Elara. I couldn't have done it without your support and guidance. Your compassion and wisdom have been a beacon of hope for the people."

Elara reached out, taking his hand in hers. "Together, we've accomplished so much. And I know that we can continue to build a future filled with hope and love."

A New Beginning

AS THE KINGDOM AND the forest continued to heal, Aiden and Elara found themselves looking to the future with renewed hope and determination. They had faced incredible challenges and made great sacrifices, but their love had guided them through it all.

One evening, as they stood on a hill overlooking the kingdom, Aiden turned to Elara, his eyes filled with love and devotion. "Elara, our journey has been long and filled with trials, but it has also been filled with moments of joy and growth. I want to spend the rest of my life with you, building a future filled with hope and love."

Elara's eyes sparkled with joy, and she reached out to take his hand. "Aiden, I feel the same. Our love has endured and grown, and I am ready to face whatever the future holds, as long as we are together."

With their hearts united, Aiden and Elara pledged to continue their quest to protect the enchanted forest and its inhabitants. They knew that their love was a powerful force, one that could overcome any obstacle and bring light to the darkest of times.

As they walked hand in hand through the forest, the trees whispered their blessings, and the magic of Eldoria embraced them. They were ready to face whatever challenges lay ahead, secure in the knowledge that their love was true and unwavering.

Together, they would forge a future filled with hope, love, and magic, their hearts bound by a bond that was as powerful and enduring as the enchanted forest itself.

The Legacy of Love

THE LEGACY OF AIDEN and Elara's love and bravery became a beacon of hope and inspiration for the people of Eldoria and Ravenspire. Their story was told and retold, a testament to the power of love, unity, and resilience in the face of darkness.

The enchanted forest flourished, its magic renewed and strengthened by the sacrifices made to protect it. The kingdom of Ravenspire thrived, its people united by a shared sense of purpose and hope.

Aiden and Elara continued their work, leading by example and guiding their people with wisdom and compassion. Their love was a source of strength and inspiration, a reminder that even in the darkest of times, light and love could prevail.

One day, as they stood by the shimmering pool in the sacred grove, Aiden turned to Elara, his eyes filled with love and gratitude. "Elara, our journey has been filled with challenges, but it has also been filled with moments of incredible beauty and growth. I am grateful for every moment we've shared, and I am excited for the future we will build together."

Elara smiled, her heart swelling with love and pride. "I feel the same, Aiden. Our love has guided us through the darkest of times, and it will continue to guide us as we build a future filled with hope and love."

As they embraced, the stars shone brightly above them, a reminder of the light and hope that guided them. They knew that their love was a powerful force, one that could overcome any obstacle and bring light to the darkest of times.

Together, they would forge a future filled with hope, love, and magic, their hearts bound by a bond that was as powerful and enduring as the enchanted forest itself.

The Journey Continues

WITH THE FOREST AND kingdom on the path to healing, Aiden and Elara looked to the future with hope and determination. They knew that their journey was far from over, but they faced it with a sense of unity and purpose.

They continued to work alongside the Eldari, witches, and knights, using their skills and knowledge to protect and heal the land. Their bond and their love remained a source of strength and inspiration, guiding them through the challenges that lay ahead.

As they walked hand in hand through the forest, they felt a deep sense of connection and purpose. They knew that their love was a powerful force, one that could overcome any obstacle and bring light to the darkest of times.

Together, they would forge a future filled with hope, love, and magic, their hearts bound by a bond that was as powerful and enduring as the enchanted forest itself.

And so, their journey continued, a testament to the power of love and resilience in the face of darkness. Aiden and Elara's legacy would live on, inspiring generations to come with the story of their bravery, sacrifice, and unwavering love.

Chapter 13: The Spell's Reversal

The Witch's Love Spell

THE ENCHANTED FOREST of Eldoria had finally begun to heal from the devastation wrought by the dark sorcerer Malakar. The village of Elarindor was thriving, and the kingdom of Ravenspire was on the path to recovery. Aiden and Elara's bond had been tested and strengthened through their trials, but one lingering issue remained: the love spell that Elara had cast on Aiden. The spell's presence still cast a shadow over their relationship, and Elara knew she needed to find a way to reverse it.

Solution: Elara Discovers a Way to Reverse the Love Spell

ELARA HAD SPENT COUNTLESS hours studying ancient texts and consulting with the Eldari and other witches, searching for a way to undo the love spell she had cast on Aiden. She was determined to remove the enchantment and confirm that their love was genuine, free from any magical influence.

One afternoon, as Elara pored over an ancient grimoire in the library of Elarindor, she came across a passage that caught her attention. It described a ritual that could reverse enchantments, restoring the natural balance of emotions and intentions. The ritual was complex and required a deep connection between the individuals involved, as well as a willingness to confront the truth of their feelings.

Elara's heart pounded with a mix of hope and fear as she read the passage. She knew that this could be the solution she had been searching for, but it also meant facing the possibility that their love might change once the spell was lifted. She needed to discuss it with Aiden and make the decision together.

Decision: Aiden and Elara Discuss the Implications and Decide to Proceed

THAT EVENING, AS THE sun set over the village, Elara found Aiden in the sacred grove, sitting by the shimmering pool that had become their sanctuary. The soft glow of the moonlight illuminated his face, and Elara felt a surge of love and determination as she approached him.

"Aiden," she said softly, her voice trembling with emotion, "I need to talk to you about something important."

Aiden looked up, his eyes filled with curiosity and concern. "What is it, Elara? You look troubled."

Elara took a deep breath, gathering her courage. "I've been searching for a way to reverse the love spell I cast on you. Today, I found a ritual that might be able to do it. It's a complex process, but I believe it can restore the natural balance of our emotions."

Aiden's expression shifted to one of contemplation. "Elara, are you sure this is what you want? Our love has grown and deepened despite the spell. Do you really think reversing it is necessary?"

Elara nodded, her eyes filled with determination. "I need to know that our love is genuine, Aiden. I don't want any lingering doubts or shadows hanging over us. I want to be sure that what we have is real and true, free from any magical influence."

Aiden reached out, taking her hand in his. "I understand, Elara. If this is what you need to feel secure in our love, then I support you. We'll face this together, just like we always have."

Elara's heart swelled with gratitude and love. "Thank you, Aiden. The ritual requires us to confront the truth of our feelings and trust in each other completely. Are you ready to do this with me?"

Aiden's eyes shone with unwavering resolve. "Yes, Elara. I'm ready. Let's do this together."

Preparing for the Ritual

THE FOLLOWING DAYS were filled with preparations for the ritual. Elara gathered the necessary ingredients and inscribed the sacred symbols on the ground in the sacred grove. The Eldari and other witches offered their guidance and support, ensuring that everything was in place for the ritual to succeed.

Aiden and Elara spent time reflecting on their journey and the love they had shared. They spoke openly and honestly about their hopes and fears, their bond growing even stronger as they prepared to face the unknown.

One evening, as they stood by the shimmering pool, Aiden turned to Elara, his eyes filled with love and determination. "Elara, no matter what happens during the ritual, I want you to know that I love you. Our journey has been filled with challenges, but it has also been filled with moments of incredible beauty and growth. I am grateful for every moment we've shared."

Elara's eyes filled with tears of gratitude. "I love you too, Aiden. Our love has guided us through the darkest of times, and I believe it will continue to guide us as we face this challenge together."

The Ritual Begins

THE NIGHT OF THE RITUAL arrived, and the air was filled with a sense of anticipation and solemnity. The sacred grove was bathed in the soft light of the full moon, casting an ethereal glow over the ancient trees and the shimmering pool.

Aiden and Elara stood before the altar, their hands joined and their hearts united. The symbols on the ground glowed with a soft, ethereal light, and the air around them hummed with magic.

Elara began to chant the incantation, her voice resonating with the ancient power of the ritual. The symbols on the ground pulsed with energy, and a surge of light enveloped them. As the ritual progressed, Elara felt the weight of the spell begin to lift, the unnatural intensity of Aiden's feelings easing away.

Aiden closed his eyes, his mind and heart open to the cleansing power of the ritual. He felt a sense of clarity and calm wash over him, the obsessive protectiveness giving way to a deeper, more genuine love.

As the ritual neared its completion, Elara's voice grew stronger, filled with a mix of hope and determination. The light around them intensified, and the symbols on the ground blazed with brilliance.

With a final surge of energy, the ritual reached its climax. The light enveloped them completely, and for a moment, the world seemed to stand still.

True Love: Confirming Their Love is Real

AS THE LIGHT FADED, Aiden and Elara stood in the quiet stillness of the grove, their hearts filled with a sense of peace and clarity. They looked at each other, their eyes reflecting the truth of their feelings.

"Elara," Aiden said softly, his voice filled with emotion, "I love you. Truly and deeply. I feel free and clear, and my love for you is as strong as ever."

Elara's eyes filled with tears of joy and relief. "I love you too, Aiden. Our love is real and true, and I am grateful for every moment we've shared. The spell is gone, but our bond remains strong."

They embraced, their hearts united in a renewed commitment to each other. The ritual had cleansed their bond, confirming that their love was genuine and free from any magical influence.

As they stood in the sacred grove, the trees whispered their blessings, and the magic of Eldoria embraced them. They knew that their love was a powerful force, one that could overcome any obstacle and bring light to the darkest of times.

Moving Forward: A Future Filled with Hope and Love

WITH THE SPELL LIFTED and their love confirmed, Aiden and Elara faced the future with renewed hope and determination. They continued their work to heal and protect the enchanted forest and the kingdom of Ravenspire, their bond and their love a source of strength and inspiration.

As they walked hand in hand through the forest, they felt a deep sense of connection and purpose. They knew that their journey was far from over, but they faced it with a sense of unity and purpose.

One evening, as they stood on a hill overlooking the kingdom, Aiden turned to Elara, his eyes filled with love and devotion. "Elara, our journey has been filled with challenges, but it has also been filled with moments of joy and growth. I want to spend the rest of my life with you, building a future filled with hope and love."

Elara's eyes sparkled with joy, and she reached out to take his hand. "Aiden, I feel the same. Our love has endured and grown, and I am ready to face whatever the future holds, as long as we are together."

With their hearts united, Aiden and Elara pledged to continue their quest to protect the enchanted forest and its inhabitants. They knew that their love was a powerful force, one that could overcome any obstacle and bring light to the darkest of times.

As they walked hand in hand through the forest, the trees whispered their blessings, and the magic of Eldoria embraced them. They were ready to face whatever challenges lay ahead, secure in the knowledge that their love was true and unwavering.

Together, they would forge a future filled with hope, love, and magic, their hearts bound by a bond that was as powerful and enduring as the enchanted forest itself.

The Strength of Their Bond

THE DAYS THAT FOLLOWED were filled with a renewed sense of purpose and unity. Aiden and Elara continued their work to heal and protect the forest and the kingdom, their bond and their love a source of strength and inspiration.

They faced new challenges and obstacles, but they did so with a sense of confidence and determination. Their love had been tested and confirmed, and they knew that they could overcome any obstacle as long as they faced it together.

One afternoon, as they walked through a sunlit glade, Aiden turned to Elara, his eyes filled with love and admiration. "Elara, our journey has been long and filled with trials, but it has also been filled with moments of incredible beauty and growth. I am grateful for every moment we've shared, and I am excited for the future we will build together."

Elara smiled, her heart swelling with love and pride. "I feel the same,

Aiden. Our love has guided us through the darkest of times, and it will continue to guide us as we build a future filled with hope and love."

As they embraced, the forest seemed to come alive around them, the trees and flowers a testament to the healing and growth they had achieved. The air was filled with the scent of blooming flowers and the gentle rustle of leaves, a reminder of the beauty and resilience of the natural world.

The Road Ahead

WITH THE SPELL LIFTED and their love confirmed, Aiden and Elara looked to the future with hope and determination. They knew that their journey was far from over, but they faced it with a sense of unity and purpose.

They continued to work alongside the Eldari, witches, and knights, using their skills and knowledge to protect and heal the land. Their bond and their love remained a source of strength and inspiration, guiding them through the challenges that lay ahead.

As they walked hand in hand through the forest, they felt a deep sense of connection and purpose. They knew that their love was a powerful force, one that could overcome any obstacle and bring light to the darkest of times.

Together, they would forge a future filled with hope, love, and magic, their hearts bound by a bond that was as powerful and enduring as the enchanted forest itself.

And so, their journey continued, a testament to the power of love and resilience in the face of darkness. Aiden and Elara's legacy would live on, inspiring generations to come with the story of their bravery, sacrifice, and unwavering love.

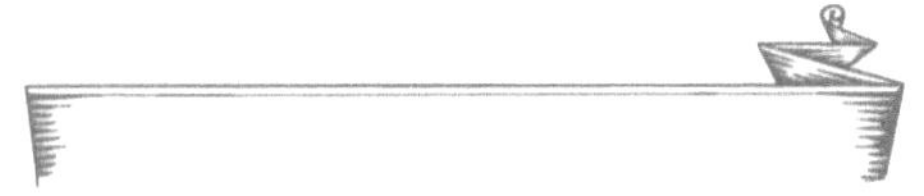

Chapter 14: The Celebration

The Witch's Love Spell

THE ENCHANTED FOREST of Eldoria and the kingdom of Ravenspire had finally begun to heal from the scars left by the dark sorcerer Malakar. With peace restored and the bond between the two realms strengthened, it was time to celebrate their newfound alliance. The people of both lands were eager to honor the bravery and sacrifices of those who had fought to protect their world and to look forward to a future filled with hope and unity.

Peace Restored: Ravenspire and Eldoria Celebrate Their Newfound Alliance

THE DAY OF THE CELEBRATION dawned with a sense of excitement and anticipation. The village of Elarindor and the capital city of Ravenspire were adorned with vibrant decorations, and the air was filled with the sounds of music and laughter. People from both realms had come together to celebrate their victory and the bonds of friendship that had been forged through their shared struggles.

Aiden and Elara stood at the heart of the festivities, their hearts filled with pride and gratitude. They had faced incredible challenges and made great sacrifices, but their love and determination had guided them through it all. Now, they were ready to celebrate the peace they had fought so hard to achieve.

The celebration began with a grand procession through the streets of Ravenspire, led by King Alden and the leaders of the Eldari. Aiden and Elara walked side by side, their presence a symbol of the unity and cooperation between the two realms. The streets were lined with cheering crowds, their faces filled with joy and admiration for the heroes who had saved their world.

As the procession made its way to the grand plaza, the air was filled with the scent of blooming flowers and the sound of music played by musicians from both realms. The plaza had been transformed into a vibrant tapestry of colors and lights, a testament to the creativity and spirit of the people of Ravenspire and Eldoria.

King Alden stepped forward, his voice carrying across the plaza as he addressed the gathered crowd. "Today, we celebrate the victory of light over darkness, the triumph of unity and cooperation over division and strife. We honor the bravery and sacrifices of those who fought to protect our world, and we look forward to a future filled with hope and peace."

The crowd erupted in cheers, their voices a chorus of gratitude and celebration. Aiden and Elara exchanged a look of pride and love, knowing that their efforts had helped to bring about this moment of joy and unity.

Acceptance: Elara is Accepted into the Kingdom, Bridging the Gap Between Witches and Humans

AS THE CELEBRATIONS continued, a significant moment of acceptance and reconciliation unfolded. Elara, a witch who had once been viewed with suspicion and fear by the people of Ravenspire, was now being honored for her bravery and contributions to the victory over Malakar. Her presence at the heart of the celebration was a powerful symbol of the new era of understanding and cooperation between witches and humans.

King Alden raised his hand, calling for silence as he addressed the crowd once more. "Today, we also celebrate the bravery and wisdom of Elara, a witch who has shown us the true meaning of courage and compassion. Through her actions, she has bridged the gap between our people and shown us that we are stronger when we stand together."

Elara stepped forward, her heart pounding with a mix of pride and humility. She looked out at the crowd, their faces filled with admiration and respect. The acceptance and gratitude of the people of Ravenspire were evident, and it filled her with a deep sense of fulfillment and hope.

"Thank you, King Alden," Elara said, her voice steady and filled with emotion. "I am honored to stand before you today and to be a part of this celebration. Our victory was not achieved by any one individual, but through the strength and unity of all of us. I am grateful for the opportunity to work alongside you and to help build a future filled with understanding and cooperation."

The crowd erupted in applause, their cheers a powerful affirmation of the new bond between witches and humans. Aiden stepped forward, his eyes filled with love and pride as he took Elara's hand.

"Elara," he said softly, his voice carrying a note of awe, "you have shown us all the power of love and unity. I am so proud of you, and I am grateful for every moment we have shared."

Elara smiled, her heart swelling with love and gratitude. "Thank you, Aiden. Our journey has been long and filled with challenges, but it has also been filled with moments of incredible beauty and growth. I am excited for the future we will build together."

Future Plans: Aiden and Elara Plan Their Future Together

AS THE CELEBRATION continued, Aiden and Elara found moments of quiet reflection and connection, away from the festivities. They walked through the sunlit glades of the enchanted forest, their hearts filled with a sense of peace and purpose.

"Aiden," Elara said softly, her voice filled with contemplation, "our journey has brought us to this moment of peace and unity, but I can't help but wonder what the future holds for us. What are your hopes and dreams for the future?"

Aiden smiled, his eyes reflecting the same sense of contemplation. "Elara, my greatest hope is to continue building a future filled with hope and love, not just for us, but for the people of Ravenspire and Eldoria. I want to ensure that the bonds we have forged remain strong and that we continue to work together to protect and nurture our world."

Elara nodded, her heart swelling with admiration and love. "I feel the same, Aiden. I want to continue our work to heal and protect the forest and the kingdom. I also want to explore the possibilities of deepening our understanding of magic and finding new ways to use it for the benefit of all."

As they walked hand in hand through the forest, they spoke of their dreams and aspirations, their bond growing even stronger with each shared hope. They talked about the possibility of creating a council that included representatives from both realms, ensuring that the voices of both witches and humans were heard and respected.

They also spoke of their personal dreams, of building a home together in the enchanted forest, a place where they could live in harmony with nature and each other. They imagined a future filled with love and laughter, surrounded by the beauty and magic of Eldoria.

One evening, as they sat by the shimmering pool in the sacred grove, Aiden turned to Elara, his eyes filled with love and determination. "Elara, I want to spend the rest of my life with you. I want to build a future filled with hope and love, and I want to do it by your side. Will you marry me?"

Elara's eyes filled with tears of joy and surprise. "Yes, Aiden, I will marry you. I want to spend my life with you, building a future filled with love and magic."

As they embraced, the stars shone brightly above them, a reminder of the light and hope that guided them. They knew that their love was a powerful force, one that could overcome any obstacle and bring light to the darkest of times.

The Wedding

THE WEDDING OF AIDEN and Elara was a momentous occasion, celebrated by the people of both Ravenspire and Eldoria. The ceremony took place in the sacred grove, a place that held deep significance for both of them. The grove was adorned with flowers and lights, creating an ethereal atmosphere that reflected the magic and beauty of their love.

The ceremony was attended by their closest friends and allies, including King Alden, Liora, and the leaders of the Eldari and the witches. The air was filled with the sound of music and laughter, and the scent of blooming flowers created a sense of enchantment and joy.

Aiden and Elara stood before the altar, their hearts filled with love and anticipation. As they exchanged their vows, their voices were steady and filled with emotion, a testament to the depth of their bond and their commitment to each other.

"Elara," Aiden said, his voice filled with love and devotion, "from the moment we met, I knew that you were someone special. Our journey has been filled with challenges, but it has also been filled with moments of incredible beauty and growth. I vow to love you, to support you, and to stand by your side, no matter what the future holds."

Elara's eyes sparkled with joy as she took Aiden's hands in hers. "Aiden, you have been my strength and my guide, and I am grateful for every moment we have shared. I vow to love you, to support you, and to stand by your side, as we build a future filled with hope and love."

As they exchanged rings, a symbol of their eternal commitment, the crowd erupted in cheers and applause. The ceremony was a beautiful reflection of their love and the unity they had brought to their people.

The Celebration Continues

THE WEDDING WAS FOLLOWED by a grand celebration that lasted well into the night. The people of Ravenspire and Eldoria came together to celebrate the union of Aiden and Elara, their hearts filled with joy and gratitude.

The festivities included feasting, dancing, and music, creating an atmosphere of enchantment and joy. The Eldari and the witches performed magical displays, their spells creating beautiful patterns of light and color in the night sky. The knights of Ravenspire showcased their skills with a series of displays and competitions, their presence a reminder of the strength and bravery that had brought them to this moment of peace.

Aiden and Elara moved through the celebration, their hearts filled with love and pride. They spoke with their friends and allies, sharing words of gratitude and appreciation for their support and friendship. The sense of unity and camaraderie that had carried them through the battle now guided their celebration, creating a sense of connection and joy that transcended the boundaries of their realms.

As the night wore on, Aiden and Elara found a moment of quiet reflection by the shimmering pool in the sacred grove. The soft glow of the moonlight illuminated their faces, and they felt a deep sense of peace and contentment.

"Aiden," Elara said softly, her voice filled with emotion, "I am so grateful for this moment, for the love we share, and for the future we will build together."

Aiden smiled, his heart swelling with love and pride. "I feel the same, Elara. Our journey has been filled with challenges, but it has also been filled with moments of incredible beauty and growth. I am excited for the future we will build together, filled with hope, love, and magic."

As they embraced, the stars shone brightly above them, a reminder of the light and hope that guided them. They knew that their love was a powerful force, one that could overcome any obstacle and bring light to the darkest of times.

Building a Future Together

WITH THE CELEBRATION of their wedding and the newfound peace between Ravenspire and Eldoria, Aiden and Elara turned their attention to building a future together. They continued their work to heal and protect the forest and the kingdom, their bond and their love a source of strength and inspiration.

They also focused on their personal dreams, creating a home together in the enchanted forest, a place where they could live in harmony with nature and each other. Their home was a reflection of their love and their commitment to each other, filled with warmth, beauty, and magic.

As they settled into their new life together, they found joy in the simple moments of daily life. They tended to their garden, explored the forest, and spent quiet evenings by the fire, their hearts filled with a sense of peace and contentment.

One evening, as they sat by the fire, Aiden turned to Elara, his eyes filled with love and admiration. "Elara, our journey has been long and filled with trials, but it has also been filled with moments of incredible beauty and growth. I am grateful for every moment we've shared, and I am excited for the future we will build together."

Elara smiled, her heart swelling with love and pride. "I feel the same, Aiden. Our love has guided us through the darkest of times, and it will continue to guide us as we build a future filled with hope and love."

As they embraced, the forest seemed to come alive around them, the trees and flowers a testament to the healing and growth they had achieved. The air was filled with the scent of blooming flowers and the gentle rustle of leaves, a reminder of the beauty and resilience of the natural world.

The Road Ahead

WITH THE SPELL LIFTED and their love confirmed, Aiden and Elara looked to the future with hope and determination. They knew that their journey was far from over, but they faced it with a sense of unity and purpose.

They continued to work alongside the Eldari, witches, and knights, using their skills and knowledge to protect and heal the land. Their bond and their love remained a source of strength and inspiration, guiding them through the challenges that lay ahead.

As they walked hand in hand through the forest, they felt a deep sense of connection and purpose. They knew that their love was a powerful force, one that could overcome any obstacle and bring light to the darkest of times.

Together, they would forge a future filled with hope, love, and magic, their hearts bound by a bond that was as powerful and enduring as the enchanted forest itself.

And so, their journey continued, a testament to the power of love and resilience in the face of darkness. Aiden and Elara's legacy would live on, inspiring generations to come with the story of their bravery, sacrifice, and unwavering love.

Chapter 15: The Eternal Bond

The Witch's Love Spell

THE ENCHANTED FOREST of Eldoria had been restored to its full splendor, and the kingdom of Ravenspire was thriving under the new era of unity and peace. Aiden and Elara, whose love had been tested by many trials, now stood at the forefront of this harmonious coexistence. Their bond, having survived the most harrowing of challenges, had only grown stronger, leading them into a future filled with promise and adventure.

Conclusion: Aiden and Elara's Love Grows Stronger

THE MORNING SUN FILTERED through the dense canopy of Eldoria, casting a warm, golden light over the tranquil forest. The sounds of birds singing and leaves rustling in the breeze created a symphony of nature that spoke to the peace and harmony that now prevailed. Aiden and Elara's home, nestled in a sunlit glade, stood as a testament to their enduring love and the life they had built together.

Aiden woke early, the soft light of dawn casting a gentle glow over Elara's peaceful face as she slept. He watched her for a moment, filled with a profound sense of gratitude and love. Every challenge they had faced had brought them closer, and their bond had only deepened with time.

As Elara stirred and opened her eyes, she found Aiden's gaze upon her, his eyes filled with warmth and affection. "Good morning," she said softly, reaching out to touch his hand.

"Good morning, my love," Aiden replied, his voice tender. "I was just thinking about how grateful I am for every moment we've shared. Our love has grown stronger with each passing day."

Elara smiled, her heart swelling with love. "I feel the same, Aiden. Our journey has been filled with trials, but it has also been filled with incredible beauty and growth. I am excited for the future we will build together."

After breakfast, they set out to explore the forest, their steps guided by a shared sense of wonder and adventure. The forest, vibrant and alive, seemed to welcome them, its magic intertwined with their love. They walked hand in hand, their hearts united in a deep and abiding connection.

As they reached a clearing, Aiden turned to Elara, his eyes reflecting the depth of his feelings. "Elara, every day I am reminded of how fortunate I am to have you by my side. Our love has weathered many storms, and it has only grown stronger. I promise to continue to cherish and protect what we have, now and always."

Elara's eyes filled with tears of joy and gratitude. "Aiden, you are my strength and my guide. Our love is a powerful force, one that has brought light to the darkest of times. I promise to stand by your side, to support and love you, as we face the future together."

Their embrace was a testament to their enduring love, a love that had been forged in the fires of adversity and had emerged stronger than ever. As they stood in the heart of the enchanted forest, they knew that their bond was unbreakable, a beacon of hope and resilience.

Legacy: Working Together to Maintain Peace and Harmony

WITH THEIR LOVE AS the foundation, Aiden and Elara dedicated themselves to maintaining the peace and harmony that now prevailed in Ravenspire and Eldoria. They worked tirelessly to ensure that the bonds between their people remained strong and that the lessons learned from their shared struggles were never forgotten.

Aiden continued his role as a leader and protector, guiding the knights of Ravenspire with wisdom and compassion. His leadership was marked by a deep sense of justice and a commitment to the well-being of all. He led by example, showing that true strength came from unity and cooperation.

Elara, with her deep understanding of magic and her compassionate heart, played a vital role in fostering harmony between witches and humans. She worked closely with the Eldari and the witches of Eldoria, sharing her knowledge and promoting mutual respect and understanding. Her presence was a source of comfort and inspiration, a reminder that love and unity could overcome any obstacle.

Together, Aiden and Elara established the Council of Unity, a governing body composed of representatives from both Ravenspire and Eldoria. The council's purpose was to ensure that the voices of all were heard and that decisions were made with the well-being of the entire realm in mind. The council meetings, held in the sacred grove, were marked by open dialogue and a commitment to finding solutions that benefited all.

One afternoon, as Aiden and Elara prepared for a council meeting, they reflected on the progress they had made. "Elara," Aiden said, his voice filled with pride, "the Council of Unity has become a beacon of hope for our people. It is a testament to what we can achieve when we work together."

Elara nodded, her eyes reflecting the same sense of pride. "Yes, Aiden. It is a symbol of our commitment to peace and harmony. I am grateful for the opportunity to work alongside you and to help build a future filled with understanding and cooperation."

The council meeting that day was a testament to the power of unity. Representatives from both realms shared their thoughts and ideas, working together to address the challenges they faced. The atmosphere was one of mutual respect and collaboration, a reflection of the harmony that now prevailed.

As the meeting concluded, Aiden and Elara felt a deep sense of fulfillment. They knew that their efforts had made a difference, and they were committed to continuing their work to maintain peace and harmony in their world.

Epilogue: Future Adventures and the Enduring Power of True Love

WITH THE IMMEDIATE threats behind them and a new era of peace established, Aiden and Elara looked to the future with hope and anticipation. They knew that their journey was far from over and that new challenges and adventures awaited them. But they faced the future with confidence, knowing that their love and unity would guide them through whatever lay ahead.

One evening, as they sat by the fire in their home, Aiden turned to Elara, his eyes filled with love and determination. "Elara, our journey has been filled with incredible moments of beauty and growth. I am excited for the future we will build together, and I am ready to face whatever challenges come our way."

Elara smiled, her heart swelling with love and pride. "I feel the same, Aiden. Our love is a powerful force, one that has brought light to the darkest of times. I am ready to stand by your side, to support and love you, as we continue our journey together."

As they looked out at the stars, they felt a deep sense of connection and purpose. They knew that their love was an enduring force, one that would guide them through the challenges and adventures that awaited them. Together, they would forge a future filled with hope, love, and magic, their hearts bound by a bond that was as powerful and enduring as the enchanted forest itself.

A Glimpse of Future Adventures

IN THE YEARS THAT FOLLOWED, Aiden and Elara continued to face new challenges and embark on new adventures. Their love remained a guiding light, a source of strength and inspiration that carried them through the trials and triumphs of life.

One spring, they set out on a journey to explore the far reaches of Eldoria, discovering new realms and forging new alliances. Their travels took them to distant lands, where they encountered magical creatures and ancient civilizations. Each adventure brought new opportunities for growth and learning, deepening their bond and expanding their understanding of the world.

In one distant land, they encountered a hidden valley inhabited by a tribe of druids who possessed ancient knowledge of nature and magic. The druids welcomed them warmly, and Aiden and Elara spent several months learning from them, gaining new insights and skills that would serve them well in their efforts to protect and nurture their world.

Their adventures also brought new challenges, including a confrontation with a rogue sorcerer who sought to harness the power of an ancient artifact for his own gain. Aiden and Elara, with the support of their allies, faced the sorcerer in a fierce battle, ultimately defeating him and ensuring that the artifact's power was used for the greater good.

Through it all, their love remained a constant source of strength and inspiration. They faced each challenge with courage and determination, knowing that their bond was unbreakable and that their love could overcome any obstacle.

The Enduring Power of True Love

AS THE YEARS PASSED, Aiden and Elara's legacy grew, inspiring generations to come with the story of their bravery, sacrifice, and unwavering love. The enchanted forest of Eldoria and the kingdom of Ravenspire flourished under their guidance, their people united by a shared commitment to peace and harmony.

Their love story became a legend, told and retold by bards and storytellers throughout the land. It was a story of resilience and hope, a reminder that true love could overcome even the darkest of times and bring light to the world.

One evening, as Aiden and Elara sat by the fire in their home, they reflected on their journey and the enduring power of their love. "Aiden," Elara said softly, her voice filled with emotion, "our journey has been long and filled with trials, but it has also been filled with moments of incredible beauty and growth. I am grateful for every moment we've shared, and I am excited for the future we will continue to build together."

Aiden smiled, his heart swelling with love and pride. "I feel the same, Elara. Our love has guided us through the darkest of times, and it will continue to guide us as we face the future together. I am grateful for every moment we've shared, and I am excited for the adventures that await us."

As they embraced, the stars shone brightly above them, a reminder of the light and hope that guided them. They knew that their love was a powerful force, one that could overcome any obstacle and bring light to the darkest of times.

Together, they would continue to forge a future filled with hope, love, and magic, their hearts bound by a bond that was as powerful and enduring as the enchanted forest itself.

Epilogue: A Legacy of Love and Unity

YEARS LATER, AIDEN and Elara stood at the edge of the enchanted forest, looking out over the thriving kingdom of Ravenspire. The sun was setting, casting a warm, golden light over the land. They felt a deep sense of fulfillment and pride, knowing that their efforts had made a lasting impact on their world.

The Council of Unity continued to guide the realms with wisdom and compassion, ensuring that the bonds between witches and humans remained strong. The enchanted forest flourished, its magic renewed and strengthened by the harmony that now prevailed.

Aiden and Elara's home had become a place of refuge and learning, where people from all walks of life came to seek their guidance and wisdom. Their legacy of love and unity inspired all who visited, a testament to the enduring power of their bond.

As they stood together, Aiden turned to Elara, his eyes filled with love and admiration. "Elara, our journey has been long and filled with trials, but it has also been filled with moments of incredible beauty and growth. I am grateful for every moment we've shared, and I am excited for the future we will continue to build together."

Elara smiled, her heart swelling with love and pride. "I feel the same, Aiden. Our love has guided us through the darkest of times, and it will continue to guide us as we face the future together. I am grateful for every moment we've shared, and I am excited for the adventures that await us."

As they embraced, the stars shone brightly above them, a reminder of the light and hope that guided them. They knew that their love was a powerful force, one that could overcome any obstacle and bring light to the darkest of times.

Together, they would continue to forge a future filled with hope, love, and magic, their hearts bound by a bond that was as powerful and enduring as the enchanted forest itself.

And so, their journey continued, a testament to the power of love and resilience in the face of darkness. Aiden and Elara's legacy would live on, inspiring generations to come with the story of their bravery, sacrifice, and unwavering love.

Don't miss out!

Visit the website below and you can sign up to receive emails whenever Sarah Elizabeth Davis publishes a new book. There's no charge and no obligation.

https://books2read.com/r/B-A-METXB-IDYIE

Connecting independent readers to independent writers.

About the Author

Sarah Elizabeth Davis is a celebrated author in the fantasy collections and anthologies genre. Known for her captivating storytelling, she crafts intricate tales that transport readers to magical realms. Raised in a town rich with folklore, her passion for fantasy was kindled early on. With a degree in English Literature, Sarah has published acclaimed anthologies, earning a loyal following. When not writing, she enjoys exploring new places and spending time with family and pets. Sarah's work, filled with wonder and adventure, continues to enchant readers and leave a lasting impact on the literary world.